True Claim

The Sigma Menace: Book Three

By Marie Johnston

Over a century ago, Bennett Young found his mate, a human woman he trusted and was brutally betrayed by. With his one chance at happiness gone, Bennett throws himself into his work. He dreads the inevitable day he turns feral and his partners will be forced to put him down, then a routine mission brings him face-to-face with his worst nightmare. A human mate. Discovering the lovely, but evasive woman is being hunted, Bennett can't bring himself to abandon her, at least not until she's safe.

Spencer King has a boy's name and lives in the boondocks for a reason. The tall, sexy shifter who showed up on her doorstep was unwelcome…and pushy. The mating instinct she feels for him threatens everyone she's worked to keep safe. Realizing the frustrating, brooding Guardian doesn't intend to leave her alone, Spencer has to figure out if she can trust him, and to decide—stay and fight, or run for her life?

To my friends and family. You were my first readers, and your enthusiasm and excitement kept me going. Thank you for all your support, your kind words, your awesome reviews, and your constructive criticism.

Prologue

1890, Kentucky

Commander Dane Bellamy stood over the woman's lifeless body while anguished screams from an emotionally destroyed male echoed in the deep recesses of the nearly abandoned mine.

"He's going to want to see her." Rhys Fitzsimmons warned him upon entering the dark control room in the small headquarters shack just outside the mine entrance.

Commander Bellamy sighed heavily. Leaning down, he wiped his blade clean on the inside of the woman's skirt, since leaving visible bloodstains would be beyond insulting to the heartbroken shifter they were rescuing.

"I know. He'll hate me, but he couldn't have lived with himself, or survived, if we let him kill her."

"He wouldn't have been able to do it." Rhys said with confidence, and Commander Bellamy firmly agreed.

Benjamin Young was crass and wild, but he'd done his best by his human wife, Abigail. Yet, no matter how tame he tried to be, she sensed the wildness inside of him and couldn't get over her fear of what he was.

Her fear was preyed upon by the local smooth-talking Sigma chapter leader and the corrupt leader's wife. Word had gotten back to them; one of their spies had known the young shifter was courting innocent Abigail. And low and behold, timid little Abigail suddenly had a new friend to confide in about her fear of her new husband. Not only his ability to change into a wolf, but his work outside of the law to police his own species.

The new friend, the Sigma leader's wife, having gained Abigail's trust, reported back to her Sigma husband after convincing the young bride to glean more information from her accommodating spouse. They used the virtuous nature of Abigail to turn her against her new husband and his entire pack.

Thinking his lovely new wife wanted to know more about the shifter Guardians' way of life and eventually commit to his world, Benji had talked with her about what their Guardian pack did, and to some extent, how they functioned.

Then on a mission that had Commander Bellamy's small Guardian pack split off into smaller teams, Benji's team was attacked. They lost two Guardians that day. Benji had refused to believe that his wife had turned on him by passing information of the mission to the Sigma leader, who then made it appear as though they had captured her. Benji allowed himself to be taken, in an effort to save her. Sigma brought the injured shifter to the faux mine, which was used as a front for the torture and mutilation of anyone Sigma deemed paranormal.

Still convinced she was innocent and that he could save his bride, Benji withstood weeks of being mercilessly tortured and studied as Abigail was used to coerce him to shift constantly, only furthering her own belief she'd married an abomination and all his species needed to be eradicated.

"At least he didn't mate her by our ritual yet. He can sense her enough to know she died, but he may still survive his grief." Commander Bellamy didn't look forward to the following months, or hell, years.

Mercury, let him out, Rhys spoke telepathically to their newest addition, an odd young shifter still learning about himself and the Guardians.

Minutes felt like hours as they waited for the distraught shifter to be helped out to the shack to say his good-byes.

Light fell directly onto Abigail's body as the door opened. A bare, bloodied, and bruised Benji shoved himself off Mercury's broad shoulders to fall at her head. He smoothed her hair and glared up at Commander Bellamy with bloodshot eyes.

"*Why?*" His heartache was gut-wrenching. "She was mine to take care of. She was *my* responsibility."

Whether Benji was asking why he killed the woman, or why he didn't let Benji kill her himself, Dane didn't know and he doubted the young shifter knew either.

"She was going to fire a shot to warn the others when she saw us. I had to stop her…" The commander drifted off, unwilling to explain how he gave Abigail a second chance to come with them, fuck, even a third chance. But when she reached for the trigger of the gun that would have echoed through the mountains, alerting Agents to descend on the mine, it left him no choice. He chose against the slower death of a slit throat, instead spinning her and shoving the blade up the base of her skull into her brain. Instant death. It was to spare Benji, not Abigail.

"I scented Agents heading this way." Mercury was calm as he informed them the enemy was closing in. He was a good addition to the pack; he would prove more vital as Benji began his healing process.

"Is the gunpowder in place?" Rhys gave a curt nod and they made their way swiftly out of the building, dragging a grieving Benji off Abigail's body.

Crouching in the shadow of the old wooden building, they waited for the commander's order to execute one of the many escape plans they came up with. The goal was to leave as few Sigma behind as possible. Mercury's power was the match for the gunpowder, but his talent had not been so reliable lately. Well, all of their talents were starting to fucking suck.

We head up, Dane communicated telepathically with his team, glancing at the rugged land surrounding them. *We can lose them on the terrain. Mercury, light 'em up.*

Mercury hesitated only long enough to concentrate on heating the kegs of powder. Blasts could be heard starting in the mines and ringing out over the trails.

They had only just begun to bolt away from the shelter of the building when a hot wall of air blasted the four Guardians out into the open.

"Mercury! You blew the building, too!" Rhys yelled, but Dane barely heard him over the ringing in their ears.

Recovering quickly as they started to take on gunfire, Commander Bellamy tried to use telepathy, but the shifters were still shaking their heads. Finally resorting to hand signals, they ran, returning fire when possible.

A grunt and the familiar smell of Rhys' blood told the commander his partner had been hit. A quick look at his pack and he made the decision they would all benefit from four legs over two.

He himself shifted, expecting his pack to follow suit. They did and the pack ran up the steep incline, weaving through the trees and brush, outrunning the human Agents. Thank the Sweet Mother for daylight, because they couldn't outrun any vampire Agents right now.

Night fell, and the Guardians kept going, stopping only for water and to catch some food, just enough to keep them from collapsing. Commander Bellamy led them on as they trudged through the night, keeping an ear and nose out for Agents, those with fangs and those without. The blasts did enough damage to keep Sigma from hot pursuit.

When the orange glow of dawn lit up the sky, Commander Bellamy gave the order to stop and regroup. Everyone in the group spread out on the ground in their human form, relaxing for the first time in weeks, all except for Benji.

One eye now swollen shut, the other red and angry and glaring at the commander, Benji finally looked away to stare blankly into the rising sun.

The weight of the world settled heavily on Commander Bellamy's shoulders. A thought he'd been batting around for a while was firmly cemented into a decision.

"Rhys," he said gruffly, "we'll make our way to the next Guardian pack and send our report to the Lycan Council." Their own meager headquarters had been compromised by Abigail. "And then I'm turning command over to you,"

Rhys and Mercury swiveled their heads toward Commander Bellamy, shock registering on their faces as they sat up. Benji continued his blank perusal of the sun.

"I'm done. I've got some shit with Irina," Commander Bellamy tried to explain roughly. Some shit was right. His mate might not despise him like Benji did, but the tragedy they both endured not too long ago caused a rift in their mating bond that he had no idea how to repair. "And Mercury still needs training, plus we'll take on more Guardians after our reassignment. They'll all need extensive training and I can concentrate on that."

Rhys grunted, nodding in agreement. "No doubt the council will stick us with rookies or fuck-ups."

It was the truth. Why this pack had the council's target painted on it, he didn't know. But the Guardians they sent were so poorly trained, they barely survived the first month.

When he became commander, Rhys would be solid, leading the pack with intelligence and little emotion. All Commander Bellamy could offer was his experience and a tenuous mating bond. The new Guardian, Mercury, whom they rescued from the wild, was still learning how to be human and had almost killed them all with his power. And Benji, a devastated shifter who hated him now, and might very well try to kill him.

Chapter One

Present day, West Creek

"He's lucky he's cute." Bennett held the squirming bundle thrust into his arms and reluctantly grinned. Every time the newest addition to the West Creek Guardian pack squalled, the lights flickered. If his mother, Dani Santini, took the time to change the hungry shifter baby's diaper before feeding him, the kid damn near blew a fuse all the way over at the lodge.

Bennett's best friend and partner, Mercury, a.k.a. Baby Daddy, was getting a handle on controlling their little Dante's powers, but there were probably a few more shattered windows in their future.

"Whatcha think, Uncle Benji?" Mercury slipped back into the old nickname he used to use before Bennett upgraded his name to outrun his past. No one needed Benjamin Young around, Grade A fool and Class A fuck up.

"I think you're not conning me into babysitting for you again." Bennett unconsciously swayed side-to-side with the tiny male swaddled in blue superhero flannel. "I just got the window and both lightbulbs replaced in my cabin from his epic tantrum the last time I watched him."

"I told you to change his diaper as soon as his face goes beet red," Mercury pointed out.

"Don't matter. He's a baby. They cry. When *he* cries, shit breaks. Little dude's got some power." Bennett handed baby Dante back to his daddy. "Besides, I've got to go talk to the new owner of the neighboring acreage. We've got reports there's some wicked traps that could get shifters out running their wolf seriously injured."

"Human?" Mercury was situating Dante into a little sling that hung over his shoulders. Bennett had damn near choked on his steak when Mercury walked in wearing the baby one morning. But it kept the little guy happy, and that kept shit from breaking. Plus, Dani swooned and got a come-hither look in her eye every time she saw her man packing baby, so everyone was a winner.

"Probably. Name's Spencer King. I'm sure he's just a crusty old recluse, trapping lunch and trying to live off the grid. But it's a threat we've got to investigate."

"Need me to go with? In case he's a crazy with a shotgun?"

"Naw. I'll just roll up for a neighborly introduction, bullshit a bit, then mention finding some traps and ask him what they're all about."

Mercury snorted. "Ya gonna bake some cookies or a nice casserole to bring over?"

Bennett scowled at his partner. "Fuck off. It's a good plan."

Mercury gave him a *sure it is* glance and strolled out of the kitchen looking like any adult woman with a ticking biological clock's wet dream, at least according to Dani. His broad muscular shoulders encased in a tight black t-shirt were easily viewed under the blue paisley fabric of the sling. Mercury's arm rested lightly under the teardrop-shaped bundle that was fast asleep.

Bennett shook his head. He'd been doing a lot of that lately, with all of the changes going on with this pack. In the last year, they gained two additional Guardians, protectors of the shifter species, with Jace Stockwell and Kaitlyn Savoy. Three if they counted the young male shifter Mercury rescued last summer. But Parrish was still young, not just young for a shifter, a literal teenager, and he still didn't talk. They all learned sign language to communicate with him, but the youngster preferred his Xbox over anything else.

Jace's mate, Cassie, had become a solid part of their pack and the psychologist was crucial to Bennett's sanity…or at least had been for a while. He got tired of talking, preferring action instead, and even that was getting old. With the twin Guardians, Malcolm and Harrison Wallace, out of the territory on official duty, he'd been loath to troll for women on his own. It had been so much easier to stroll into the backrooms at the shifter club, Pale

Moonlight, where the twins were working their magic on random women, and join in.

For years, he'd been the recruiter, leading nubile sex partners to the notorious rooms dubbed The Den, where he and other shifters exorcised their demons through extreme physical exertion. It got old. It really did. Unmated shifters, especially Guardians, needed an outlet for their increased levels of aggression. Fighting only went so far, maybe a little therapy helped, and then there was sex. And that wasn't helping like it used to. Not the random, nameless hookups he'd been having, and with the twins gone, it left…expectations…when it was just him. The girls would want to kiss, touch, and, ugh, talk.

He used to go to The Den with Mason and Mercury. But Mason's downward spiral beyond major asshole was halted when his heart got blown out of him, and Mercury was solidly mated to the human, Dani. And didn't that just stick in Bennett's craw.

Of course he was happy for his partner and best friend. Maybe he couldn't find a human woman who accepted him for what he was, willing to turn her back on everything she knew for life with the Guardians, but he was happy Mercury found one. After the suggestion by their nemesis, Madame G, that Mercury could choose his own mate, she wasn't predetermined, well…it just rankled a little more.

Seeing Jace and Mercury each in their respective forms of mated bliss left Bennett feeling…conflicted. They both found human mates who not only left their lives as they knew it, but dedicated their themselves to defending the shifter species. Over a century ago, Bennett had been happily married. Or so he thought until his human mate was brainwashed, told that someone like him was an evil abomination and needed to be destroyed, with her help.

Abigail was weak, mentally and physically, and her humanness was the only comparison that could be made to Mercury's and Jace's mates.

But why wasn't Bennett worthy of a solid, quality mate? And wasn't that the number one question that had been riding him hard for the last one hundred and twenty-five or so years?

The other question was: what the hell was he going to do? He'd taken on increased responsibility and was now second in command to their pack leader, Commander Rhys Fitzsimmons. Their pack was facing off with the local Sigma chapter under the rule of the demented, evil Madame G. Suspicions of corruption in their own ruling body, the Lycan Council, left their pack short-staffed while the twins were sent off to investigate.

Finding a mate was a once in a lifetime event. Urban legend suggested that shifters who didn't go off the deep end when a mate was lost to them, could find another destined to bond with, if they lived long enough. But finding substance to the myths never went beyond "my cousin's best friend's dad's old roommate heard of a guy who…"

So here he was. He'd survived the devastation of his mate's betrayal and her subsequent death, or execution, as it were, thanks to his duty and Guardian brothers. However, he was finding it increasingly difficult to control the raging emotions roiling in his chest and old memories banging around his head. He was so. Damn. Angry.

Giving his head a brief shake, he ran a hand through his short blond hair, making sure it was tousled just right. One secret to his survival had been to alter his name and looks, distancing himself from that guy. That guy who was stupid enough to believe a timid, human woman would remain by his side, endure his duty, and welcome him home into their bed after a suckass day. The aww-shucks Benjamin Young with the scruffy good looks and dusty cowboy hat became the immaculate Bennett Young, who wore expensive shit and never had a hair out of place. Benji—fucking loser. Bennett—winning.

Time to go see an old crusty bastard about some traps.

***

What a nice spread.

A good three hundred and twenty acres sat next to the Guardian's land. Both chunks of land were far enough away from city limits to be considered extremely rural and isolated. The Guardians kept tabs on all the land owners around their acreage. There were just a few owners really, and only one wasn't a shifter. The previous non-shifter owner was okay letting the land grow wild, snoring loudly all night while shifters freely ran his property, and heading into town to hit on the silver-haired ladies at the senior center all day. It was an ideal situation until the guy hadn't shown up in town one day and the senior center ladies called the local police, concerned about him, and found he'd passed away quietly one night.

The new owner might be an issue. Recently, shifters exercising their wolves in the woods had some near misses with steel traps. Concerning enough, until Kaitlyn came back from inspecting the traps claiming they were plentiful, covering the entirety of the property like land mines.

Driving down the ambling, dusty road that served as a driveway, Bennett decided at the last minute not to pull too close to the house. If he was in his furry form, the fur would be standing up on the back of his neck. Instead, he parked on the circular drive so he was angled toward the exit and protected by the SUV when he stepped out.

After he climbed out, he let his senses soak in the surroundings. Birds were singing, enjoying the sunny spring weather after a harsh winter. Two cows stood in a pasture, a good hundred yards from the main house. Who the fuck only had two cows?

Bennett spun when he heard a screen door open and resisted the urge to transition when a large German shepherd slammed the door open the rest of the way. Growling and snarling, the beast roared toward him, fangs bared.

Without hesitation, Bennett flung out a mental command. *Halt!*

The beast stopped abruptly, already midway between the house and Bennett. He swung his furry head toward the house where a figure stood shadowed in the doorway, and then the dog made a lunge back toward Bennett.

Mentally, Bennett held the large dog in place, grateful his erratic ability was steady today. He rarely used his gift. Seriously, who needed to talk to animals? And how long could one guy put up with Snow White references? All of his pack's gifts had been increasingly unstable for the last century, so much so they'd become less and less dependent on them almost to the point of disuse. That is, until the last year, when some of them started finding mates. It seemed as if their powers became stronger and more grounded with each mating. Bennett thought that meant he was screwed.

The German shepherd whined and sat with a huff on his haunches, then turned his head back to the house.

Keeping his hold on the loyal dog, Bennett took in the figure that walked out.

Shiiiit. His chest grew tight; his breathing became shallower. Not due to the shotgun emerging from the doorway, thankfully pointed downward, but it was the arm attached to it. Bennett ran his eyes up from where the tanned hand confidently gripped the shotgun barrel, up the delicately muscled arm encased in a red plaid shirt to where the rolled-up sleeve showed off a slight bulge of bicep. His eyes continued up the sun-kissed skin of a slender neck, bared by a clip holding up the sun-bleached, honey-brown hair, letting it cascade down from the clip like a waterfall of ripened wheat. Bennett took in the lash-lined hazel eyes and full, raspberry-hued lips and felt like he'd been punched in the gut.

Because it wasn't the stunning beauty, cautiously stepping off the porch, suspicion ripe in her bright, intelligent eyes that made Bennett feel like he was suffocating. It wasn't the glinting steel weapon in her hand or the dog trained to attack.

No. The bottom dropped out of Bennett's world as soon as he caught the scent, drifting toward him on the gentle breeze. The scent of lavender and vanilla, the signature smell of this human female. The scent of his mate.

Chapter Two

N o. No, no, no, no, no. Son of a dried up, moldy biscuit. This wasn't good.

Not only was there a towering male standing in her driveway, and her ferocious Cuddles was somehow rendered useless, but this wasn't just any male. She knew immediately he was a shifter, one used to wielding power and authority, *and* he was her destined mate.

Fudge.

"Can I help you?" Spencer called, standing at the base of her porch steps. She whistled for Cuddles to come to her side and stared in astonishment as her dog swung his head toward the male, who gave an imperceptible nod of his head, warning in his deep, navy blue eyes. The movement would've been undetectable to most people, but she wasn't most people.

This male didn't know she wasn't an ordinary human female, and that's the way it needed to stay. She stole another moment to size him up while Cuddles trotted to her side and took up a stance in front of her, facing the stranger.

He was tall. Like, really tall. She was five-three and he had to be at least six-five. His white-blond hair had the I-just-rolled-out-of-bed-this-sexy look, but she was sure it was styled. The yuppie clothing confirmed her suspicion—leather loafers, sleek button-up shirt, and designer jeans. He gave the impression he was going out clubbing instead of taking a Sunday drive in the country.

Spencer felt the male's second sweep across her body like a burning brush fire. His expression, no doubt reflecting her own, with equal parts suspicion, dismay, and intrigue. Good, she could use that. She had no room in her life for a shifter mate, and if this male felt the same way, the sooner they parted, the better.

Switching on obvious charm that didn't reach his wary eyes, he smiled and the bottom plunged out of her stomach. Holy Smoky Bear, he was lethal. And that smile, directed her way, made it seem like he was attainable and willing, like he stepped out of a cologne ad just for her.

"Howdy, ma'am. I just stopped by to introduce myself."

The male started forward, probably to shake hands. And as much as the thought of touching him skin-to-skin made her palms sweat in anticipation, she needed to make him stop.

"You can make introductions from there."

He stopped abruptly, his eyebrows rising in surprise. Again with the devastating, but fake, smile.

"Yes, ma'am. I'm Bennett Young. Pleasure to meet you, Miss…?"

"Why are you here?"

Again with the eyebrows rising. Maybe he was used to getting what he wanted, especially out of women.

"We're neighbors, ma'am. Just fixin' to introduce myself." Where before she thought she heard a hint of southern drawl, she was sure of it now. And sure that he was forcing it, authentic or not. Maybe that worked with most human women, heck, it probably worked with most species of female, but she wasn't normal and as much as she wanted to roll in the syllables slipping off his tongue, she couldn't afford any kind of weakness now.

Wait, did he say neighbors? Aww, nuggets.

She grudgingly gave in. "Spencer King."

There go those eyebrows again. She shocked him three times now and found she liked catching this male off guard.

"You're...? Miss King, it's my pleasure."

Really? Because it didn't look like it. It looked like she had kicked his puppy and told him the Tooth Fairy wasn't real. He probably assumed the new owner was a guy and was expecting to bypass the difficult woman. People assumed Spencer was a guy's name, that was exactly why her parents named her that. Usually she went by Sarah, but Spencer knew this male would keep pushing until he talked to the new owner.

"Nice to meet you, Mr. Young. Thanks for stopping by." Spencer backed up to head back inside without taking her eyes off him.

He made a move forward. "Please, call me Bennett. How are you liking it here?"

A low rumble emanated from Cuddles and was cut off immediately. Brows drawn, she checked over her dog but nothing seemed amiss. Cuddles was shooting Bennett a look of consternation. Bennett himself was gazing innocently back at Spencer.

"It's fine," was all she said.

"My buddies and I live on the bordering property, to the south. We're in real estate and finance. We like the privacy to work."

Suuure. "So you and a bunch of guys set up a *commune* for finance and sell real estate?" Oh, sugar. Even as she said it, the meaning dawned on her.

A bunch of male shifters living far from town. If they all resounded with the same intensity and power this male did, she knew exactly what they were. Who they were. Guardians. *Smooth move, Spencer. Way to fly low and innocuous.* No wonder land records didn't alert her when she researched this place. They probably bought it under a dummy name years ago.

"No, not like that. We have women, too. I mean, shit…" He blew out a breath of frustration.

"I'd appreciate it if you watched your mouth on my property, Mr. Young," she said primly.

Rising eyebrows and a slow blush almost made her smile. She was beyond a hat trick for shocking him, and moved on to embarrassment. Or pissed off, she wasn't sure yet.

"I apologize, ma'am. I was just trying to clarify our living situation so as not to alarm you."

"No need," Spencer attempted to brush him off. "Thanks for the info. See ya around." Attempt number two at getting up her porch steps to send a clear message to Bennett that the conversation was over.

He took another few steps in her direction. Cuddles tried to growl again, only to get cut off, thumping his tail in frustration against the ground.

"Miss King, I see you have cows. Are you turning this place into a hobby farm?"

Spencer's lungs froze. He was asking about her cows. Why did he need to know about her cows? Deciding a modicum of truth was the best policy, and maybe the fastest way to get him the heck gone since he was obviously searching for information, she quickly deliberated what to tell him.

"Yes, Mr. Young, though Bessie and Tulip are more like pets."

The devastating smile flashed. "Bennett, please."

"Bennett." Oh, that felt too good rolling off her tongue. Did his navy eyes just sparkle with satisfaction? "I plan to have a hobby farm of sorts, but also grow and sell for retail."

"Do you hire in help, or do you have a family out here to help?" Subtle. She didn't miss the calculating look in those mesmerizing eyes.

It didn't take long for her to decide what to tell him. His heightened senses would know she was the only one out here. She could pretend to have a beau, but she had enough to hide without adding extra facets to her story.

"I'm independent. Perhaps I'll expand this operation eventually, but as you can see, I'm just in the beginning phases now that it's spring."

"I'd love to hear more about your plans. Care to grab some coffee?"

"I don't drink coffee."

"A soda, then."

Scrambling mentally for a suitable excuse to avoid further alone time with the drool-worthy male in front of her, she glanced back at her rundown, shoddy house. When she turned back to Bennett, she released a small gasp. That brief second she took her eyes off him he used to cover the distance between them.

Cuddles gave a small growl and Bennett looked at her protector sharply before holding out a strong, work-roughened hand. To her astonishment and utter dismay, Cuddles granted Bennett a little sniff before bumping his head under the hand. Before, her beloved dog may have been under some kind of compulsion, but now he was just a desperate softie.

"What's his name?" Bennett asked fondly, scratching the pooch behind the ears.

"Cuddles."

Bennett blanched and gaped at her with alarm. "*What?* And he tolerates it?"

"He should. He earned it," Spencer said a bit defensively. Every time she ceased movement and so much as sat down, she was covered in a giant mound of panting fur. She even had to upgrade bed sizes so she at least had a little room to sleep around the massive German shepherd.

"It should be, like, Maximus or Apollo, or something manly. Not fu-, ah, Cuddles."

It disconcerted her that she was pleased he cleaned up his language for her. "You can ask him what he prefers and call him that, but to me he'll always be Cuddles." His demeanor turned calculating and she realized her error. "I'm sure he'll be full of suggestions, like most males." She attempted to play it off as a joke, like she didn't suspect he was controlling her dog. "I'm sorry, Bennett. I'll have to take a rain check on the soda. The weather forecast is excellent today, and I need to get some work done."

Bennett scanned their surroundings and she knew what he saw. Old gardens, overrun with brown, dried weeds and brush and dilapidated fences that were missing entire sections. The previous owner let the surrounding woods encroach on the cleared acres that had once been used for farming and ranching. The house itself had been allowed to wither under age and weather, but was structurally sound, for the most part. Sometimes the amount of work was more mentally overwhelming than physically. But she had time.

"Well," Bennett drawled, putting Spencer back in his sights. "I'll hold you to that rain check. How 'bout I lend a hand around here?"

This close, she could see the flecks of lighter blue streaking through the navy in his eyes. Backed by the bright sky, he had an avenging angel beauty. The light of his hair reflected the sun's rays, the shadows highlighted the masculine planes of his face.

Tamping down the bloom of arousal that had been persistent since she met him, she again attempted to brush him off. Persistent Guardian. "What a thoughtful offer." Good job, she kept the sarcasm out of her voice. "But your clothes would be trashed in two minutes. Don't worry about it." Spencer put her hands on her hips, a note of finality in her voice. "I'd better get back to work."

Refusing to squirm as her movements stretched her top tightly around her breasts, attracting his instant perusal. She was grateful the morning chill in the air made her throw on an over-shirt, but she'd only buttoned it halfway, and her white tank top had a low neckline allowing the top swells of her breasts to be on display.

"Let me go change and I'll be right back." Before she could argue, he was heading back to his SUV.

Uh, no. "No need, I'm fine." She resisted the urge to run after him, feeling like she could finally take a full breath now that there was distance between them.

"No trouble, Miss King. I'll be back." He hopped into his vehicle and pulled away.

Fiddlesticks. Looking down at Cuddles, who was giving her a questioning look, and then at the shotgun in her hand, she realized her best defenses might well be useless against Mr. Bennett Young.

Chapter Three

"She's my worst nightmare."
Bennett sat at the table in the lodge's kitchen, elbows on the top, hands buried in his hair, while he slumped over trying not to hyperventilate.

He'd held it together on the drive back. Even sent out a summons to meet with the commander and Mercury upon his return. He filled them in on everything, not that there was much, but there was certainly enough. Now both Commander Fitzsimmons and Mercury sat across the table from Bennett, dumbfounded.

He knew the feeling. His own mind could barely process registering the sense of his mate after well over a hundred years, the drop-dead sexiness of the woman, and that she was human. The one thing it processed clearly was that she was hiding something, and he needed to find out what.

"Dude, that's fucked up. Another human mate?" Mercury was baby-free, taking advantage of naptime and leaving Dante with his mate in her office.

"Thanks, Captain Obvious." Bennett sat back in his chair with a huff.

"Go help her out, see if you can get her to open up. Investigate what you can." Commander Fitzsimmons was not the person to go to for sympathy. The male was much older than him, yet the score was two-to-zero for mates. The commander was the most intense, formidable male he knew, and Bennett hoped to see the day he found his mate, to see the kind of female it would take to make the stolid Rhys Fitzsimmons beg for a belly rub. But…every so often, Bennett had a sneaking suspicion he knew why the commander wasn't mated and it might not be because he hadn't found her yet.

"I can't go back there," Bennett admitted miserably.

Both males sat across from him, silent. The commander raised an eyebrow expectantly.

Bennett pushed away from the table. "I'll go get changed and head over there."

"Watch yourself, bro. Check in every hour." Mercury didn't like the idea of Bennett going over there, either.

"She's just a human," Bennett scowled.

"So was Abigail and she almost killed all of us."

Fucking Mercury. He had a habit of saying what he shouldn't, but sometimes, it was what needed to be said the most.

***

Old t-shirt, check. Work jeans, check. Raging hard-on every time he pictured sparkling hazel eyes, unfortunately check.

Pulling in the driveway at Spencer's place for the second time that day, Bennett shut off the SUV and hopped out. Cuddles bounded up to him, tongue hanging out. He'd won the dog over, now for the owner.

He pinned Cuddles with a sharp gaze. "Seriously, dude. Maximus or Apollo?"

Deep brown eyes regarded him for a moment before Cuddles let out a short bark.

"Apollo it is. Where is she?" Spencer. Hell of a name for a girl. What were her parents thinking?

Apollo hesitated, giving him a soft whine, still loyal to his human.

Bennett held his hands out to the side with a shrug. "I'm only here to help."

Apollo turned and loped off, Bennett followed.

He saw a straw hat hovering above a particularly nasty set of dried out weeds. Spencer was pulling from the base, slowly clearing a patch of land for a nice sized garden.

Bennett got the distinct impression she knew he was there and was choosing to ignore him. Pulling on a pair of leather work gloves, he stationed himself next to her and went to work.

"I told you not to come," she said, without skipping a beat in her clearing.

"No, ma'am. You said 'don't worry about it' so I'm not worried about coming to help."

That made her stand up, looking all cute and exasperated. The big hat shaded her face and neck, her red plaid shirt was still on and what he would give to see her in just that white tank top.

"Well, thank you," she said with a clipped tone. "I'm going to take these to the compost pile."

He continued pulling weeds, peering through them to watch her rounded bottom as she bent over to gather her work from the previous hour. Then he had to stand up and readjust before stooping back down to work.

They continued like that for hours. She didn't offer to stop for lunch and he didn't mention it. But he was fucking starving. It felt good to toil away under the hot sun. It's what his people were made for. Demanding work tending to Mother Earth, then cool off running their wolf through the shaded woods.

His duty could be physically challenging at times, especially if there was fighting involved, plus they did their own manual labor around the lodge and cabins. Most times, it was a lot of driving and investigating, as they were the police force for their people, and they had a wide region to cover in addition to the West Creek/Freemont area.

Bennett's ears picked up on metal snapping against metal before he heard the yell of pain.

"Stay here." he ordered, before he took off at a sprint into the surrounding trees.

The sprint slowed quickly when he almost ran into one of his sexy neighbor's metal traps. Concentrating on dodging them and keeping his senses open, he detected the taint of a Madame G recruit.

Son of a bitch! He hoped Spencer listened to him and stayed put. He didn't need to reveal himself to a human, didn't need her to witness the ruthless side of his nature as he disposed of the recruit, and didn't need to waste his time on explanations.

Making a wide circle, stepping silently through the budding trees, he came around behind the young male recruit.

"Guys!" the recruit was whisper-shouting through the trees. "Help me get my foot free. Guys?"

Little bastard didn't realize he was disposable to both Madame G and his buddies. Wishing he had time to interrogate him, he sent mental information to Commander Fitzsimmons and knocked the man out. Now, to find the others.

Crouching low, he slid a knife out from one boot and followed his nose to the putrid smelling recruit who was trying, but failing, to hide behind a tree. This one had a set of binoculars and was peering through the trees toward the direction of the house. Good luck seeing anything through the trees, idiot. But what was he looking for? Did the recruits think Spencer's land was part of Guardian headquarters?

Since he had already left one recruit in the trap for interrogation, this one could be disposed of. He clamped his hand over the man's mouth and slid the knife through his ribs straight into the heart. It wasn't until he was laying the body down he realized it was a set-up and he'd taken the bait.

The impact burned as a bullet pierced Bennett's thigh. Yanking his knife out of the fallen recruit, he threw it with deadly accuracy toward the shooter. Not waiting to find out if he hit his target (he knew he would), he ignored the fire in his leg and bent to retrieve another knife to take on the recruits rushing toward him from different directions.

There were two and he was injured. The odds weren't bad, until one pulled a gun and took aim at Bennett's chest like he actually knew what he was doing. Bennett was twisting to the side, readying the second knife to throw, when the blast came. The recruit's body, peppered with holes, was thrown sideways. Spinning to take on the other attacker who was almost upon him, he slowed when Apollo jumped the recruit from behind and tackled him to the ground.

Silver glinted in the underbrush, aiming for Apollo's belly.

Apollo, back! Bennett commanded, jumping between the dog and the recruit. He easily wrestled the knife away and buried it into the recruit's chest.

Standing slowly, pivoting toward where the shotgun blast had come from, he stopped when he found Spencer. Her hat had been knocked off, the hair clip had fallen out, and her hair hung in loose waves down around her shoulders and back. She was magnificent, and pointing her trusty shotgun at him.

Apollo growled, racing to his companion to protect her. The other Guardians were closing in.

Wait! He didn't want them revealed yet.

Spencer swung her head to each side, as if she knew where the hidden shifters were.

"Do you know these men?" she demanded, holding the barrel tighter.

"Well, now..." Bennett spoke low and calmly, his bloodied hands in the air, "maybe if you took your aim off me, we could talk."

She clearly didn't want to, but finally lowered the barrel to the ground, still holding it like she was prepared to shoot.

"Do you know who these men are?" he countered.

"Of course not," she said defensively. "I moved out here to avoid the crazies."

"And the traps?"

Panic flashed through her eyes. She gave him a quick once over, eyes lingering on his bullet hole. "You're injured."

"Just a flesh wound," he lied. It was more than that, but no major arteries were damaged; he'd heal quickly. "Let's head back to your house. I'll call my friends to come help clean up."

She paled, clearly not liking the idea. "Aren't you going to call the police?"

Taking a gamble that she wouldn't want authorities involved due to whatever she was hiding, he bargained, "I won't if you won't."

"Did I kill him?" Spencer asked, lifting her gun slightly in the direction of the one she shot.

Yep. "He's down for a while. My team will take care of him." As in burn his body.

"What were they out here for?"

Bennett sifted through stories to tell her. "Nothing good, especially for a young woman living alone." Spencer went ashen, so he chose to elaborate on something just as believable. "Poachers probably, maybe drugs, who knows? They were bad men."

She tossed him a dubious look as if she hadn't decided whether Bennett was one of the good guys or not. Glancing around at the bodies of the recruits, she appeared to struggle with the next step to take. "What about the one in the trap?"

To give her the impression the recruit in the trap was no threat to her, Bennett shrugged her question off, deciding to go for cover story number two. "My buddies and I were all in the military before we left for less stressful work, but we still have connections. We'll take care of it. Let's get back to your house."

Ex-military my round bottom. Spencer tromped back toward her house. As far as fake background stories went, there were worse ones. Most people never really thought about what special op guys did after they retired, and finance and real estate wouldn't likely be questioned. No one assumed a former military badass would hang out working a nine-to-five job, attending PTO meetings.

Still, she was grateful the other Guardians were going to take care of the bodies. It wasn't the questions about why the men showed up in her backyard, or about the traps she was worried about. Those could be thrown back at the males. She could use their fake cover story of being ex-military against them, because then they certainly had to have enemies and should understand the traps were to protect a single woman living in the country, working the soil with her hands.

No, what was making her blood pressure spike was the thought of Bennett in her house. Bleeding. He'd better heal the heck up. Perchance she'd catch a break and he wouldn't leave the rich, masculine scent of his fresh blood lingering in her domain and the rancid smell of the recruits' blood would be enough to cover what had already dried on his pants.

Taking a deep cleansing breath, she let Apollo in the house and followed him in, letting the door shut in Bennett's face. It was rude, yeah. He took care of three immediate threats, was arranging clean-up, and she should be grateful, throwing herself at him, asking what she could do for her big, strong man.

Instead, she was irked he'd ingratiated himself into her life after less than a day, threatening her sanctuary of isolation.

Not that it was a sanctuary anymore. Maybe those recruits really were looking for the Guardians, trying to gather information. But what if they weren't? What if they'd found her already? She was sick of running, sick of hiding. This was her chance at finally living, albeit off in secrecy, but with a home. An identity.

Bennett faced her after entering her house, leaned against her counter, his arms crossed. His natural woodsy scent, mixed with his rich blood, was making her light-headed. Their close proximity, standing together in her mud room, increased her awareness that she was closed within four walls with her mate.

She needed him to go. "You'd better get back to your place and take care of that wound."

"Why, Miss King, aren't you going to patch me up?"

Oh lawd, he was trying her patience. She wouldn't put it past him to drop his drawers so she could tenderly care for his wound. Giving herself a mental snort as a distraction from the realization that he probably didn't have underwear on, she concentrated instead on her increasing irritation. And hunger.

"I'm no good with that stuff. I might pass out." And she would, but not for the reason he thought.

"We can't have that." His voice deepened and she felt his penetrating gaze on every inch of her body. "Then you'd be at my mercy, instead of the other way around."

Heat flushed through her and she grew very, very aware this tall, gorgeous male was supposed to be her mate. They were supposed to be at each other's mercy, over and over and over.

"So, why were those men out there with guns? Did you make enemies while you were in the service?" She fervently hoped her questions would cut the sexual tension and deflect any assumptions that she was the target.

She was rewarded with only a slight decrease in intensity from the virile male.

"I'm sure we did. Any reason they'd be after you?" His scrutiny became even sharper; she resisted the urge to squirm.

Trying not to outright lie, he'd sense her deceit, she phrased her answer carefully. "I could only guess. But I am alone out in the country, and that's reason enough for many bad guys. I would think you and your friends were the most likely target."

"Uh-huh." Well, he didn't buy it, but maybe he'd drop it. "Why the traps?"

Shoot. "Again, single woman out in the country. I can't chance an animal attack, and I can't fence the whole property."

"Uh-huh. There is a numerous amount of traps."

"I have a lot of land. When I get my gardens in, I can put in ones for rabbits, and put up deer fences. I'll be getting some cats, too."

"What about Apollo?"

"Who?"

"Cuddles," Bennett's voice practically dripped with distain. "There's no way I'm calling him that. Aren't the traps a safety hazard for him?"

Spencer rolled her eyes. Men. "He gives them a good sniff, and he's with me when I set them up. He'll be fine. You should go take care of your wound."

They were at an impasse and he wasn't budging. His blood was going to drive her insane. Her heart pounded with each beat, her vision going double. It wouldn't be long before she attacked him. Sliding past him without touching him, she opened the door.

"I'm not feeling well." She didn't have to lie about that one. "I need to rest after today's excitement."

Bennett's jaw clenched, his intense gaze still on her. With predatory grace, he moved in front of her where she was holding the door open.

"I'll come check on you later," he murmured quietly. He towered over her so she had to crane her head back because she absolutely refused to step back. Honestly, she didn't know if her body would listen to her brain's command to put distance between them.

"No need." She was trying to be firm, instead she sounded breathless.

Staring into the deep blue depths of his eyes, neither one of them moved. Not even when he slowly dropped his head down to catch her lips with his own, giving both of them plenty of time to change course.

It was the first time they touched and it was *electric*. Her lips tingled where his touched. The pressure increased, now his hands were on her, settling on her hips, drawing her in close. She let go of the door and grabbed his t-shirt, twisting her hands in the warmth of the material.

His tongue swept across the seam of her lips, coaxing them open. She greedily accepted him. His scent surrounded her, amplifying his male, virile flavor. A shower would wait, at the very least, this shirt she wore that's been smashed into him wouldn't get washed. Golly, how her loneliness sunk in when she plotted how to retain his smell long after he left. She didn't know how much time passed while they stood there kissing, reveling in the taste of each other.

Abruptly, he broke away, stepping back and looking horrified, before he stumbled out the door at a near run.

Mind blank, the decadent taste of him still on her tongue, she watched the dust cloud kicked up as he drove away.

Chapter Four

"**D**ude, quit being a pussy."
Mercury was an asshole. Bennett ground his teeth together and flipped off his partner. Their functioning emergency doctor, Garreth, was extracting the bullet with what felt like a pair kitchen tongs. The pain was a welcome diversion from the haze of lust and dismay he'd been in when he arrived.

Mercury came to brief him, while Commander Fitzsimmons had a nice little chat with the recruit from the trap. The other bodies were smoldering in their fire pit, but the marshmallows would have to wait.

"There we are." Doc Garreth flung the bullet in the garbage. He set about wiping off Bennett's leg and slapping a bandage on while he gave instructions. "Drink water, have a big steak, and leave the bandage on for at least a few hours so you don't bleed all down your leg."

"See ya, Doc. Thanks." Bennett trashed his pants and threw on one of the many pairs of shorts stashed around the lodge, handy with injuries and the after-shift nakedness.

Giving a little wave as he hobbled out with Mercury, Bennett mused how his leg had hurt less when he showed up than it did after he was treated. Doc Garreth was indispensable, though. Before Mercury rescued him from Sigma's compound, the Guardians did their own down and dirty emergency surgery. The pain might be the same, but recovery was now faster.

"Any info yet? Or are you just following me because you like my ass in these shorts?" Bennett asked Mercury, heading to the kitchen. Missing lunch and losing blood were making him cranky. It had nothing to do with the scent and flavor of his luscious little mate lingering on his lips and his clothing.

"You have a nice ass, but I'm following you because I want to know what's wrong."

"What's wrong is *her*."

Entering the kitchen, he went straight for the fridge to dig meat out.

"It's your turn to cook tonight," Mercury informed him, folding his arms over his chest, watching Bennett.

Fuck! He forgot. Growling, he dug out more steak.

"Spill it." Mercury wasn't going to give up.

"I kissed her."

"No way!"

Mercury's shocked expression made Bennett feel better. He knew his friend would understand. He hadn't kissed anyone since Abigail. She had ruined intimacy for him. Hell, ruined women. They were of no use to him except to scratch the itch. He turned on the charm to lure them in and then let them go after he got what he needed. No drama, no fuss.

Mercury jumped in to help prepare the meal, probably taking pity on Bennett hobbling around, wanting to talk with him more before the others showed up to eat.

"She's not Abigail."

"No shit. Abigail wouldn't have picked up a gun, much less blown someone away."

Spencer had saved his ass. Sure, he would've recovered from another bullet wound, after his team dragged his sorry butt out of there. But then to her, he would've been dead. He wasn't going to examine his feelings too closely at the possibility of having to stay away from her, or even worse, tell her what he really was.

"Just sayin'," Mercury said. "Might not be a bad thing that Spencer can do that."

"She's hiding something and we don't know who she is." Bennett didn't want to entertain the idea of actually taking this mating business seriously.

"Well, proceed with caution. But don't write her off because she's human."

"Do you charge per hour, Dr. Phil?"

"You're a dick. Want me to throw her in the holding cell like you did with Dani?"

Bennett growled at the idea. Mercury was making a point, and yeah, maybe he did that to the male's mate, but he had good reason thinking she was a Sigma Agent at the time.

"That's what I thought."

Bennett ignored Mercury, and after he finished grilling and devouring a couple of steaks, he left to find their young shifter Guardian, Parrish. Mercury had rescued him from Madame G's clutches several months ago, at the same time he broke Doc Garreth out, but the male still didn't talk. Bennett could go for hanging out with a mute right about now.

In the game room, sitting in front of the Xbox as usual, Parrish was absorbed in a *Call of Duty* mission. Perfect. Grabbing a controller, Bennett flopped on the couch next to the pale-haired male who automatically set up a two-player game so they could both get their kill on.

After an hour, or three, Parrish abruptly stopped the game. Without turning to Bennett, he signed, *You need to go to that club*.

"Pale Moonlight?"

Maybe Parrish heard about the club from the Guardians, but he certainly wasn't old enough to visit. It was the last place Bennett wanted to hang out right now, even though it should be the first place he went full of so much emotional turmoil. "Why?"

Just feel like you should go.

"And do what?" Bennett asked, while his fingers tersely snapped the words off while signing. There was nothing wrong with the kid's hearing, but it was easier to stay fluent if they signed in return. It was unlike the teenaged male to be pushy. Sullen and withdrawn, absolutely. Not pushy.

The boy just shrugged, giving Bennett the impression that he really didn't know. A wave of relief went through Bennett. He wasn't so far gone that even Parrish wanted him to go bang females until he felt better. Not that he wouldn't like to release himself into a willing female's body. However, there was just one female on his mind and he wouldn't be tangling with that filly any time soon.

For now, a little virtual battle and maybe a *Die Hard* marathon would have to do.

***

Bass reverberated through Bennett's skull. He let it wash through him, hoping it would take some of his aggression with it on its way out. He'd spent the last few weeks getting nagged by a mute teenager to go to the damn club.

Getting more and more wound up each day wasn't helping. He stayed far away from Spencer's land and hadn't ventured to town for a little sexual healing. He didn't dwell too long about the reason why, but it certainly wasn't because he would feel like a gigantic jackass to be with other women while his alleged mate was only miles away. That absolutely wasn't the reason. He gave *everything* to his first mate and almost lost more. Fool me once, Bennett thought bitterly.

Unfortunately, *Halo*, *Call of Duty*, action flicks, and extreme training only went so far. Working off his hostility in the training center helped, especially since Kaitlyn and Jace were now fully trained Guardians. He could take on both of them and sometimes get his ass handed to him so well that he spent a blissful afternoon recovering without feeling like he was going to implode.

But here he was at Pale Moonlight. Two women, regulars, had already asked him if he was heading to The Den. Shit, had he taken them more than once? That showed how clouded his thinking had been in the past year if he violated rule number one—sex with the same woman more than once in the same night was okay, but never, ever again after that. Otherwise they started getting ideas. The word "relationship" began to taint their thinking.

At least rule number two was safe. Always from behind. No touching, no kissing, and definitely no embracing. Bennett didn't want arms twined around his neck or legs wrapped around his waist, just needed to work them from behind and help them get the hell out so he could start again with a new girl.

The old system he and Mercury and Mason had developed worked really well. The late Guardian warmed up the ladies with the touchy-feely stuff and after he released himself he handed them over to Bennett and Mercury. Then Dani came into Mercury's life and he dropped down like a two-hundred and thirty-pound ball of whipped male for the woman. Bennett suspected his odd friend would've been toast even if Dani hadn't shown up pregnant with his child from a Sigma insemination meant to deliver Madame G her very own shifter baby. In fact, Mercury even said he was enthralled with the human before he caught the scent of his young within her.

Why the evil Madame G needed her taint on a baby, they hadn't figured out yet. While the Guardians were working on that, they investigated why Mason betrayed his own pack, and to figure out if the betrayal went as deep at the Lycan Council, the ruling body of shifter kind.

The twins, Malcolm and Harrison, went north to investigate the council, while the others stayed in West Creek to focus on taking down Madame G and her chapter of Sigma. Shifters would never win the battle over the Sigma menace if their own governing body was causing festering wounds within the packs themselves.

It sucked the twins had to go. They weren't pillars of personality; Harrison barely talked and was extremely touchy, but he worked well with Malcolm's magnetism and charm. Which attracted the females both he and his brother enjoyed, often together.

Bennett hung his head down staring into the amber depths of his Belgian ale, remembering how he'd been successfully dealing with his emotional baggage by getting his head examined by Jace's human mate, Cassie. The woman was a psychologist, and after mating with Jace, her natural talent blossomed into something more powerful. Yet, she wasn't strong enough to heal Bennett's damage. So one night, when he stumbled into the club's back bathroom and found Malcolm thrusting into a girl from behind, while his brother was sitting on the counter getting head from her, well…Bennett found a new system that worked for him. Even better, Malcolm did the footwork, finding willing bodies, freeing Bennett from practicing his false charm.

But the twins had been gone for months and now Bennett had ninety-nine problems and a woman was definitely number one.

"'Bout time you came in." Christian Williams slid onto the bar stool next to Bennett and faced him.

The tall, dark shifter was not only the owner of Pale Moonlight, but pack leader of the shifters employed at the club. Most of the shifters were rejects from other packs, lost souls who found their way to Christian and into his motley crew. The club served to provide not only employment, but catered to the increased sexual needs of the unmated in their species. Bonus, the increased shifter traffic sometimes brought mates together.

Scowling at the thought of mates, Bennett redirected his attention to the intimidating male next to him and lifted an eyebrow. "Been looking for me? I know, I'm a stud, but you're taken."

Christian snorted. "Mabel wouldn't care if you were a guy, she'd kick my ass, and then yours if I even thought of checking you out."

True. Mabel was tiny, but Bennett wouldn't cross her. Christian might rule the club, but she ruled him, and Bennett suspected Christian was just fine with that. In the years they'd been in West Creek, he'd seen enough women and men, both shifter and human, drawn to the muscular male with smooth, dark skin and mesmerizing black eyes. The austere owner blew them off, always, and if they kept bothering him, then he cut his mate loose on their sorry ass. After that, it was end of story.

"What's up?" Bennett was curious now. If Christian had pertinent intel to pass on, he usually notified the commander.

Christian leaned back against the bar, resting his elbows on the surface, facing the crowd. Tilting his head, he aimed his voice toward Bennett, speaking low. The male had the handy ability of throwing his voice so only those who he intended could hear. Speaking quietly in a loud club to a shifter with heightened hearing didn't work because all shifters in the club had heightened senses.

"One of my pack that works here caught on to a Sigma spy who keeps coming in. A guy, a young and preppy human, keeps asking weird questions to the girls he hits on."

"Like what?"

Christian scanned the crowd again, his black eyes almost shimmering. "You sit there and look all pretty and let me talk."

Bennett set his mouth in a hard line and resisted rolling his eyes. Pack leaders were major assholes.

"First, he'll ask questions to determine if the girl is a shifter or not. That always sends up warning flags and I turn the guy over to Rhys." Christian and the commander had formed a tight working relationship. The Guardians would use the information to negate any threats to their kind and do it in a way that didn't lead back to the club so Sigma spies kept coming in.

"If the girl's human, he moves on. But if she's a shifter, he keeps on with the questions, all suave-like, trying to find out their parent's names, where they're from, if they have any siblings."

Bennett flashed Christian a droll look. The questions were odd only in that the club was a place to hook up and this guy seemed to be looking for lasting love.

Christian pinned Bennett with a dark stare. "Check the attitude, Guardian. I'm getting to the good stuff." Casting his gaze around the room he continued. "All the women have the same look— petite and fair. Dude never takes them to the back, only wants to talk. We've kept an eye on him and noticed the women jerk their arm back at least once after he touches them. That's when my guy noticed the ring."

Okay, now the story was picking up.

"After each girl, the ring changes, sometimes color, sometimes design, like he switches it, but we haven't actually seen confirmation. Then he whips out his phone like he's texting, but one of our servers got a peek and saw he was making notes of all the information he'd gathered."

Bennett was about to ask one of the twenty questions he had, when he got silenced by glittering black eyes.

"I know you're bursting with questions, and I'm getting to it." Christian shook his head. "Man, why couldn't Rhys have come in first. Dude lets me finish. Here it is. He's definitely looking for a particular woman. No, we don't know if he's Sigma, but my guess is yes. Yes, he still comes in, but hasn't in several days. Of course I'll give you his description."

You need to find her. The words echoed in Bennett's head as surely as he heard them spoken again by the supposedly deranged young man hiding in a psych ward. The Guardians had tried to gather information from him a few months ago. The guy claimed Sigma was after his sister. He had stared directly at Bennett when informing them they need to find the mystery woman before Sigma killed her.

"Word is, he's not the only one hunting a woman." Christian was full of information tonight. "One of the bouncers at one of the other clubs in Freemont heard some women chatting about getting hit on by a hot guy who did nothing but ask questions."

Bennett let the information sink in as he gazed across the bar counter, using the mirror behind the bottles to scan the club behind him. So, they were trolling the whole area and if they've deployed that many spies, then they knew *she* was here, but didn't know who she was either. Regardless, Sigma knew more than Bennett.

Well, it was time to hit the town.

Chapter Five

I *don't want to go in.* Spencer sat in her truck outside of the country western bar her acquaintance arranged to meet her at.

The young woman Spencer had gotten to know owns a small store with her husband that sells homemade goods in West Creek. They were looking to add locally grown seasonal produce and Spencer was working hard to get recruited by them. It would be the perfect set-up. A secure client to sell to, who could mediate between her and the public, without Spencer putting her face out there. She could create a steady income and remain mostly anonymous.

But first, she had to go into this place. A public place, with loud music that would dull her senses, with all kinds of strangers bumping into her and even worse, noticing her.

With a resigned sigh, Spencer opened the door of her beat-up farm truck and slid out. Her cowboy boots made minimal noise on the concrete walk leading up to the popular bar and grill in West Creek called Boots Up. There was no debate between boots or heels, or boots with heels. Spencer was not only a country girl, but a smart girl, and heels were beetle dung for running. Paired with her worn jeans and purple plaid top, she would either integrate superbly or be horribly out of place.

Spencer paused just inside the door to take in the scene and gather her wits. This was so far out of her comfort zone.

Rustic chic was the theme with wood as far as the eye could see. Wooden beams lined the walls and ceiling, lacquered logs for tables and wooden booths sat on top of a polished cherry wood floor.

As for the social scene, Spencer noted everything from her own style of dress, some with cowboy hats, to slinky dresses and tight leggings. Perfect. Blending in was pertinent and this would do. The crowd seemed to lean toward couples and groups. Even better.

"Hey Spencer, you made it!" Her friend Constance bounded up to meet her, calling Spencer by her real name. Her parents had said that under different circumstances, they would've named her Sarah. Since a girl named Spencer attracted more attention and unwanted questions, she usually just went by Sarah for casual acquaintances. Since she didn't have anything more than casual relationships, almost no one knew her real name.

Except for Bennett, the frustrating Guardian. And now Constance and her husband. She worried her desperation for a connection to society was making her careless.

Constance Smythe and her husband, Mark, were five or so years older than Spencer, she'd guess thirtyish. The couple had embraced the locally grown, organic, no-GMO, no additives, all natural lifestyle, and were currently spurring enthusiasm from the community to make their living providing the qualified products.

Spencer wove through the bar, following Constance to a booth where her husband waited. They spent the next couple of hours chatting about the produce Spencer could grow, the timeline of her stock, and prices. Spencer nailed it thanks to the 'shrooms. Not recreational, not therapeutic, but to put on salad and in spaghetti sauce—button and cremini mushrooms. They weren't hard to grow, just a little tedious.

The mushrooms would kick-start her growing season, with her herbs, until the bigger produce started coming in. Constance and Mark were impressed with Spencer's knowledge and confidence in her products and the growing season. Spencer easily played it up like it had always been her family's way of life, something she'd grown up doing. It was…sort of true. Natural talent filled in the rest. A natural talent with nature not many humans could claim. Spencer used it carefully, but shamelessly.

"I can't wait until your first delivery!" Constance exclaimed. "We'll come up with a contract and call you so we can meet up and you can go over it."

Mark extended his hand. "Looking forward to working with you."

Spencer shook his hand. She could see herself getting to know these people. Actually be friends or something.

"We'd better get going. The sitter texted me. She forgot she has a test tomorrow, so we should call it a night." Constance slid out of the booth and leaned in to give Spencer a quick hug before they left.

Spencer rested back in the booth and watched them walk out, hand-in-hand, content to see a happy couple, even though that ideal wasn't in the cards for her. But maybe dessert was. Everyone here had already seen her, so she was one of the crowd, and it had been ages since she had lava cake. She signaled the server, put in her order, and relaxed back to wait, trying not think about her friendly neighbor. Why couldn't she get him off her mind?

A shadow fell over her booth.

Aww, heck.

Ideas of a peaceful dessert faded into obscurity when her heart rate picked up for the grim, blond, mountain of man standing by her booth, dressed much like the first time he showed up at her place.

"What brings you here, Bennett?" Was he meeting friends? Or worse, a date? Anger spiked harshly within her. It was obvious he was ignoring the fact she was supposed to be his mate. What if he did more than ignore it?

That…teed her off. And that feeling was irritating. She was ignoring the mating call as much as he was, having no room in her life for further complications.

"Just hanging out." Bennett took the seat across from her, resting his arms on the table, hands folded, regarding her quietly. "You?"

Just hanging out. He was full of dookie Whatever, it wasn't her business and for once she didn't have to lie.

"I was meeting some future clients and decided to stay and have some dessert."

"Clients for what?" he asked bluntly. Gone was the charming neighbor, tonight Bennett was somber, tampering down his fierce energy, keeping it coiled tightly while he scanned the crowd. His eyes would land on any couple sitting and chatting, wait a heartbeat, and then move on to the next couple.

"I plan to grow fruits and vegetables and sell them at local markets. Maybe even have some internet orders."

Those navy blues landed on Spencer and her breath hitched. He was an intense male, and he was completely focused on her.

"You really think you can make a living doing that?" The sardonic tone grated on her.

She wore her most coy expression. "Why, Mr. Young, do you doubt my ability?"

"I'm sure you can grow whatever you want, but enough to make money? Through our winters, and with your land surrounded by trees?" His look intensified. "You don't plan on cutting down the trees do you?"

Horrified, Spencer shuddered. The trees were her shelter, keeping her hidden and safe. "Of course not. There are more ways to make a living off the land than razing it for mass production."

"Fill me in then." Bossiness was second nature to this male.

"First of all, there's my little babies, the mushrooms. Then the berry and grape plants I'll start. Wine's big nowadays, so maybe I'll dabble in that. Herbs grow fast, and drying them and selling seasoning packets will be good winter income. Then there's the standard tomatoes, potatoes, carrots, cucumbers, pumpkins. Lots of options."

The lava cake was slid in front of her by the college-aged male server. He grinned at her delight and received a heavy scowl from Bennett.

Unintimidated, the server turned to Bennett. "Can I get you anything, man?"

"Whatever pale ale you have on tap." A quirked eyebrow at Spencer had her shaking her head.

"Just water, please," she said.

The server left to fill their order and Bennett resumed his scrutiny of her.

"Hitting the hard stuff tonight?"

"I had Diet Coke earlier, so I'll be jittery all night as it is."

Spencer continued to dig into her cake, sliding the second fork the server was thoughtful enough to provide, toward Bennett. He glared at the fork like she poisoned it, before picking it up and swiping a bite.

"Shit's good," he said around his mouthful.

Spencer glowered at him.

"What's your thing with swearing?" He kept swiping bites from her cake, his scrutiny on her lips wrapping around the fork. It should've made her uncomfortable. Instead it made her feel...powerful.

"There's enough ugliness in life, I don't need cussing to make it worse."

Nearly rolling his eyes, but abstaining, he watched her devour her warm chocolate deliciousness. He shifted in his seat, his jaw clenching.

Once Spencer scooped up as many crumbs as she could rescue, and licked them off her fork, she set the fork down and excused herself to go to the restroom. All the soda and water was building up.

Wrapping up in the ladies' room, she maybe straightened her hair a little more than normal, adjusted her shirt, and turned sideways to check out her butt in the mirror. Ridiculous. She wasn't going home with Bennett so her looks didn't matter.

Breezing out the door, the same server gave her friendly smile. "How's it going?"

"Oh, uh, fine."

"You're new here, right?" He was punching in order info at a little console.

Stiffening, Spencer shot him a quick smile, acting like she was in a rush back to her booth and hadn't really heard him.

Weaving through the bar, she spotted a tall, willowy blonde saunter up to Bennett. His eyes were following Spencer, oblivious to the woman.

Spencer's ears picked up the woman's throaty question. "Hey, remember me?"

Bennett's brow furrowed as he glanced at the beauty. "Sorry?"

"From the club, over in West Creek. We hooked up a couple of months ago." The woman now sounded a little strained, like she shouldn't be explaining who she was to someone who apparently knew her intimately.

Bennett's face paled. Instead of watching Spencer approach, he glanced down at his beer. "No, sorry."

The woman shifted, unsure for a moment, before kicking her hip out and thrusting her chest forward a couple of notches. She leaned over the table and purred. "Why don't we head over there? I'll make sure you don't forget me again."

"No, thanks."

Spencer finally reached the booth and plopped in. The woman shot a glare her way before swinging her determined attention back to Bennett.

"Come on. It's not too late," the woman tried again.

"Honey." Spencer cut in, cringing at the thought this scene could get ugly fast. The girl's insecurity was like a badge on her shoulder. "You're clearly beautiful, he's clearly a player. Don't you think you deserve better?"

Both Bennett and the stranger turned shocked looks her way.

"Excuse me?" the woman half-asked, half-challenged.

"You deserve a guy who spends one night with you and is smitten. Like, make your bed, take out the garbage, cook you dinner, smitten. You should never, ever, have to remind any guy who you are."

The stunning blonde blinked rapidly at tears the unexpected onslaught of emotion Spencer's words had wrung out.

Standing up fully, tugging down on her minidress, the woman squared her shoulders. "Well lady, those kinds of guys are a myth."

"If you're looking for them in bar they probably are," Spencer countered. "What do you enjoy doing? That's where you'll meet someone."

The woman huffed and hastily brushed more tears away. "There's not many hot guys in the church quilting circle."

"No," Spencer pondered. "But how many of those mad quilting grandmas have single grandsons?"

Chuckling despite herself, the beauty gave Spencer an appreciative smile. "You two have a good night. And…make him work for it."

Bennett looked like he was going to have a stroke. When the woman was gone, he ran a hand through his perfectly mussed hair.

"She seemed nice." Spencer directed her teasing tone toward the disconcerted Guardian. "I didn't catch her name. What was it?"

Better to cut things off before they started. "I never did get her name either."

A delicate eyebrow rose, and fuck, Spencer was trying not to laugh at him. Most other girls would've been, *should've been*, disgusted with him. A human girl especially should be throwing her drink in his face and storming off with Random Hookup Girl to dish about how men suck.

He pressed on, might as well lay it all out then and there. "I've been known to frequent clubs occasionally for quick sex with anonymous women. All night long."

A pretty blush stole across her features, but her surprise seemed to be more about his admission than what he was actually admitting to.

"Have you ever gotten any of their names?" Her tone was still teasing, but he detected a hint of curiosity.

"One, and she's a complete pain in my ass."

"My kind of girl." Spencer's sass never ceased to amaze him. "What's her name and why didn't things go anywhere with you two?"

"Kaitlyn and I weren't looking for anything to go anywhere. Now she's a coworker of sorts, and my company has a strict no fraternization policy." There was no concern about any lingering feelings between Kaitlyn and Bennett other than the dose of respect and friendly affection he held for his fellow, spunky Guardian.

"So, is that why you're out tonight? For anonymous sex?" Her voice was soft, as if she was afraid of his answer.

Seizing the opportunity to destroy a budding relationship with this woman who was supposed to be his mate, he wore his most serious expression. "Yes."

A fleeting look of bewilderment preceded her utterance. "Liar."

Well, that backfired. "I'm not the only liar at this table."

"I have never lied to you. We hardly know each other enough to lie." Oh, she was cute angry. The fire lit the green hues in her hazel eyes making them sparkle.

"You said you didn't know those men in the woods." Granted, he hadn't smelled her lie but it didn't mean she wasn't hiding something. The recruit they had captured expired before any useful information was pried out of him, though they did find out he wasn't out there targeting Guardians.

"I didn't."

"Okay. Why were they after you then?" Let her answer that with no scent of deceit.

"I doubt they were after me."

Well, now. There it was, the scent of a lie. Spencer King knew there were men searching for her. Did she know they were Sigma?

"Have you ever heard of an organization called Sigma?"

"Nope." She was the poster child for innocence.

But she was lying. Lying about the knowing the men were after her, lying about knowing about Sigma. Here he was, out hunting for men looking for a fair and petite woman, and he ended up with a fair and petite woman who had men looking for her. And both groups of men were affiliated with Sigma.

Coincidence? It couldn't be.

"How's your brother?"

Blood leeched from her face. She nervously glanced around and grabbed her purse, making a move to go.

"Spencer, wait."

"I need to go."

The server appeared at the booth, blocking Spencer's escape. "Hey there guys. How was everything?"

"Oh sugar! I almost forgot the bill." Exasperated, Spencer rummaged through her purse, but Bennett beat her to it throwing some bills on the table.

"Thanks, man." The server pocketed the money, not taking his eyes off Spencer, even while walking away. "You two enjoy the rest of the night."

Bennett gave the server a closer look. He seemed...off. Could he be gathering information for Sigma? An employee would be a good way to find single women and ask them random questions. He should see if the man wore a ring.

No time now though. Spencer exited the bar.

Bennett trotted to catch up with her, but not too fast. The roll of her hips those boots gave her in those jeans—*day-um*. Her hair hung loose down her back, a silken fall a guy could bury his face in when he thrust into her from behind.

The painful erection he associated with this little human made itself known. Spencer stiffened and she glanced over her shoulder as she walked.

"Thanks for buying me dessert. I'll talk to you later," she called back to him.

"No, Spencer, we need to talk now."

"Sorry, I gotta get home. Cuddles—"

"Apollo is fine. Talk to me now, or I'll follow you home, Spencer."

She slowed to a halt, feet from a truck that had seen better days, or hell, better years.

"Fine. We'll talk in my truck, then you can leave."

"Do you always park next to dark alleys?" What was the woman thinking? She had people after her and *this* was the spot she chose?

A stricken look crossed her face as she scanned around. "It wasn't dark when I parked here," she said lamely.

"Get in."

Bennett waited until she shut the door before walking around the front to the passenger side. Slowing in front of the alley entrance, he cocked his ear to listen into the darkness.

As he climbed into her truck, he examined the extended cab while she glared out the windshield.

"I happened to be out tonight looking for some men that were brought to my company's attention. They work for Sigma and seem to be hunting a woman. Want to tell me why?"

He didn't think she was going to answer him. Studying her profile, he was struck by her natural beauty. Sun-kissed hair framed a face that required no makeup, a natural blush highlighted her bronzed skin, and long eyelashes rimmed her brilliant, intelligent eyes.

If he was receptive to being mated, this woman was a fine specimen, despite her secrets. Too bad he'd rather go feral and be put out of his misery before facing that heartbreak again.

"I thought you were in real estate?" she challenged.

"I think you know I'm not," he countered.

"Tell me first what you know of my brother."

Clever move. "Ronnie, if that's his name…hell, is Spencer yours?"

"Yes." That's all he was going to get.

"Ronnie Newton is locked up in a padded room at the psych ward in Freemont's hospital. He's a hard guy to talk to, but he told me I needed to find his sister before Sigma did." He closely watched as her jaw clenched and unclenched with his words. Her eyes fell closed and when she opened them again, she continued to glare out the windshield.

"We don't know why they're after me. They seem to think I mean bad news to their organization."

"How long have you been in hiding?"

"The last twelve years or so. When I was thirteen, my grandparents were killed along with my aunt, she was only eighteen. We didn't know why until my family was attacked, and it seemed they were targeting me. My parents, Ronnie and I got away and went on the run, and I've been in hiding ever since."

"And you don't know why it's you specifically?"

Spencer paused, formulating her words. "We've heard varied reasons, but none of them make sense."

"Be honest, Spencer. You know about us." It wasn't really a shot in the dark, and it would explain a lot about her trust in him taking care of the bodies at her farm. Most human's first words after something like that would've been "call" and "police." She uttered those words half-heartedly after a bit of chit-chat.

With a sigh, she slumped back in her seat. "You mean, have I learned about other species in this world? Yes."

"And I am?" he prompted.

She finally faced him, her gaze sweeping his face. He liked her perusal. "Since I talked with you in broad daylight, I would guess you're a shifter, not a vampire."

It was like a huge boulder lifted from his shoulders. The burden of keeping his non-human status a secret while helping her ate at him. He would've been anticipating the tearful denials and hysteria that followed an eventual revelation.

But here she was. Sitting in a truck cab, announcing that she knew of his world, and there was no disgust on her face.

Before he realized what he was doing and to stop himself from such a monumental error, he leaned over to take her lips with his own.

Her startled gasp opened her lips enough so he could sweep his tongue inside. Twining his tongue with hers, he reached over to haul her across the cab and onto his lap. She settled on top of him, her knees straddling his hips, her hands running through his hair while his reached around to cup her top-notch ass.

His erection was killing him. Leaning back so he could thrust up into her jean-clad valley, he attempted to ease the pressure by rubbing against her center. Spencer ground down against him, rocking with his movements.

Moving his hands from her delectable bottom, he glided them up her slender waist to cup her supple breasts through her shirt.

Moaning into him, his responsive little mate was making the most erotic sounds. The sensation of her rocking on him…better than anything he had experienced in a long time. Fuck…in forever. If she kept that up, he would put prepubescent adolescents to shame and cream his own shorts with nothing more than a little clothed heavy petting.

He thumbed her pert nipples through the soft fabric and she rode him faster, he arched higher into her. Deeper, he plundered the sweet depths of her mouth, chasing the end waiting for them both; the sweet ecstasy of coming in a mate's arms.

If Bennett was in his right mind, he wouldn't have allowed this. Absolutely not, not with touching, not with kissing, and certainly not without penetration. But the feel of this woman drove his common sense away.

A shocked gasp tore Spencer's mouth away from his before she cried out her release. The sight of her wanton ecstasy pushed Bennett past his limits until he came in his pants, grateful to have chosen the dark denim designer jeans to pair with his forest green pullover.

This was too much. *She* was too much. Swiftly, but gently, he set her in her seat, and without meeting her eyes, turned to get out of the truck. They could talk later about her situation, on the phone or something.

"Sit your derriere back down," Spencer commanded.

Pausing with the door ajar, he looked back at her.

"What's your issue, anyway?" Turned in her seat, her eyes were full of fire while her cheeks were still highlighted with desire. Stunning. "You skedaddled the last time you kissed me and now you're going leave a cloud of dust in your haste to get out. What's up?"

"Look, Spencer—"

"Don't give me the 'it's not you, it's me' spiel. I know that, don't try to blow wind up my behind. This isn't the last time we're going to see each other, *friendly neighbor*. So talk."

A smile crossed his lips, completely unbidden. Her candor was refreshing, but he wasn't going to dive into his sordid past with this little human that made his mating senses tingle. He had one shot at happily ever after and now it was gone. No need to row that boat again.

"I was married once," he began, not just using the human term for Spencer's benefit, although she might be familiar with mating if she knew about his species. He'd agreed to a legitimate marriage ceremony, in a church, for Abigail's sake, to help her accept him and his nature. "She tried to accept me, she really did. But a smooth-talking Sigma leader coerced her to turn me in."

"You were captured?"

"Yep." Bennett exhaled a gusty breath. The betrayal always felt recent, though many decades had passed. "My pack freed me, and they almost got killed in the process. She ended up being killed in the crossfire." That was the nice version. There was no accident with her death, and no amount of time would lessen his guilt.

"When was that?"

"Before the turn of the century."

Spencer narrowed her eyes on him. "Which century?"

She knew about their lifespans, too. "Early nineteen hundreds."

"How old are you?"

"I'll turn two-hundred and eleven this year."

"Let's see if I can try to fill in the blanks. So you found your mate pretty young and she proved too mentally weak for your kind of life. Your relationship went down in flames, so now you won't let any woman get close to you."

Um…yeah, but so much more complicated than that. "Pretty much."

A sound from the alley grabbed Bennett's attention seconds before prickles of awareness rippled over his skin.

"Fuck! An Agent. Stay here and lock the doors."

Spencer watched as Bennett crouched outside the pickup, then rose with a wicked looking knife in each hand. Where was he hiding those? She'd been pressed pretty closely to him just minutes ago.

Even under the dire circumstances, the memory of riding his hard length, with her tongue down his throat—or was his down hers? Okay, either one made her flush all over again. Her breath quickened as she stared at the male stalking the alley entrance.

Before he shut the door, Spencer had caught the stink of vampire and was completely okay sitting in the truck while Bennett hunted fang. Maybe the Agent was after the Guardian and not her.

Bennett knew her brother, had talked to him. Spencer's hope that she could find him, and bring him with her into obscurity, were dashed when she learned of his confinement in the psych ward. *Sugar!* She couldn't leave him there, but she couldn't very well break him out, or even visit him, without sending out alarms alerting them to her location.

What if she told the Guardians her story? What if her telling them jeopardized her parents' anonymity? Or her brother's well-being? What if they wanted to use her to get closer to Sigma? Guardians were notorious alpha males and could trod over her wishes easily. No, it wasn't worth it. She would need to keep her distance from Bennett, both emotionally and physically, and protect her secret in order to keep her family safe.

Spencer's sharp ears picked up on sounds of a scuffle deep in the alley. Debating on whether or not to move the truck, and aim the headlights down the alley to light-blind the vampire, a knock on the window made her jump and let out a girly shriek.

"You okay?" The server from the bar called through the window.

A hand on her chest, feeling her heart churn underneath, she gave a reassuring smile and wave.

He made a motion with his hand wanting her roll down the window.

"I'm fine," she called through the closed window, unwilling to open it. "Have a good night."

The server smiled again, meaning to reassure her and shook his head, putting his hand up to his ear like he couldn't hear her. What a crappy time to get hit on.

She shook her head again and gave him a dismissive wave. His smile stayed in place, but his eyes darkened. Next thing she knew, she was looking down the barrel of the black gun he held.

Her reflexes kicked into action. She jerked the door handle and shoved the door open hard and fast into him, knocking the gun out of his hand. He stumbled back in surprise. Closing the door immediately and locking it, she started the truck, threw it into gear, cranked the wheel, and floored it.

Realizing he'd better move or he'd get run over, the server gave up on finding the gun and stumbled back as the truck swung out to the side toward him.

Moving out farther than she intended, and passing him, she threw the lever into reverse to back over the gun or the server, but she saw in the review mirror that he'd already recovered his gun and was pointing it at her through the rear window.

Before Spencer could step on the gas in an attempt to hit him before he got a solid shot off, a dark form flew into the server, tackling him to the ground.

Double sugar snap! Now she couldn't see either one in the mirrors or windows, they were wrestling on the ground too close to her pickup.

Bennett rose up, like an avenging angel in the glow of her taillights. His hair still mussed from her hands, his clothes rumpled with dark stains, and that fierce male beauty of his spurred desire ahead of her fear.

Meeting her eyes in the mirror, he jutted his chin out to her in question. Nodding that she was okay, he first looked around to determine if there were any witnesses before he bent and hauled the server's body up and threw it into the back of the pickup.

Planning to voice all kinds of arguments about why she couldn't have a dead body in her pickup, she opened the window.

Bennett started talking before he was even in front of her. "We'll drive around to my car and I'll transfer him and dispose of him."

"Sigma?" Raking her gaze over him to see if any of the blood was his, she detected mainly the stench of tainted vampire blood. If Bennett had been injured, he must be healing already.

"I don't smell it on him, but it's too much of a coincidence that he's after you as soon as an Agent shows up. Did he talk to you tonight?"

"Other than taking my order, no." She had thought the server seemed like a nice guy. "Wait. When I came out of the bathroom, it seemed like he wanted to strike up a conversation. Asked if I was new to town, but I kept walking."

Bennett nodded like her news confirmed his suspicions. He was inspecting a weird-looking ring he pulled off the man's body.

He pocketed the ring and looked up. "Spencer, have you heard of the Guardians?"

Nodding, dread filled her belly.

"You need to come stay with us, we can protect you and find out why they're after you."

"No way."

"Spenc—"

Holding up her hand, irritation flashed across his face as she shushed him. "I get it. I'm in danger. But I'm tired of running. I don't want to be driven off my land, and especially not at a critical time for starting my business."

He opened his mouth to argue again, so she rushed on. "I promise I will lay low. I promise to call if there's any problems. But Bennett, I'm not running anymore."

The finality of her declaration had him grinding his teeth as he considered the situation.

"Fine. Follow me then."

"What about the vampire?"

"Dusted." He glanced toward the alley, not speaking for a moment. "Wait here. When I come out of the alley, follow me to my car."

Bennett walked around the front of the truck and disappeared into the alley. Spencer rolled her window up most of the way, to keep aware of her surroundings.

One minute ticked by, then another. *What is he doing?*

Alarm started to rise in her gut until his tall form sauntered out of the entrance carrying a beat-up cardboard box.

He refused to look her way as he walked down the street, expecting her to follow him.

Instead, she pulled up next to him and opened the passenger window. Catching a fetid scent. *Really?* "What's that?" she asked amused.

"Kittens," he bit out a bit defensively.

"Where's the mama?"

"Dead."

Huh. Her heart melted just a bit and she so did not need that around this alpha male.

"How do you know?"

Using his key fob to unlock a black car, he also opened the trunk before sliding the box into the passenger seat. "Just do," he finally replied. "Bar's going to close soon. We need to get out of here."

After the body swap was carried out, Spencer followed Bennett and his pack of felines, suppressing a giggle at the thought. Kittens. And he gave her a hard time about the name Cuddles.

She followed him all the way to her place with no incidents. He pulled in and helped her hose the blood out of the pickup bed, then waited until she was safe in her house before he pulled away.

Chapter Six

Slumping against her locked front door, she huffed out a big breath. She had a lot to contemplate—her new supplier contract, the attack, her planting schedule. One thing she would not be thinking about was a brooding, blond shifter who kept popping up and gave her the best clothed orgasm she ever thought possible. It might even rank up there with the best orgasm ever.

Like any red-blooded woman, she liked sex. She liked it more because of who she was, but she reined in her urges, occasionally venturing out for a quick hookup. Relationships were out of the question, and she never stayed in one place long enough to revisit the same bed twice, so to speak.

If she were to visit the Guardian's bed, she had a feeling she wouldn't want to leave it. Son of gun, she was thinking about him. Back to the produce contract.

Prepping for bed, Spencer tied her hair back and scrubbed her face before changing into flannel pajama bottoms and a thin, long-sleeved t-shirt, all the while mentally running through growth charts and planting schedules.

Cuddles' warning bark and the purr of an engine pulling up her drive brought Spencer to the door to grab her shotgun. She peered out the window. *What the h-e-double hockey sticks?*

A familiar black sedan pulled in next to her truck and out hopped Bennett. She watched his lithe body, now dressed down in black sweat pants and a black t-shirt, stride around to the passenger side to grab a duffle bag and the beat-up cardboard box.

Swinging the door open, she waited for him to approach. A male like him holding a box full of kittens he'd rescued tightened her chest. She tamped down the desire that flared because she couldn't tear her gaze away. Cuddles gave a curious whine, but after a scowl from Bennett, the dog was satisfied to sniff at the box as Bennett came closer.

"Something wrong?"

"Yeah." He maneuvered past her. "You won't stay under our protection, so I will have to stay with you."

Seconds passed as shock sucked the air out of Spencer's lungs, and she was helpless to watch as he wandered farther into her house, looking around.

"You can't stay," she finally sputtered out.

"Sure I can. If you don't have Wi-Fi, then we may have an issue, but I'll solve that soon enough." Little mews came from the box. "Where's your guest room?"

"I don't have one. I have seedling and mushroom rooms until I can get the basement ready."

"You've got a couch. That'll do."

The infuriating male strode to the couch and dropped his bag. Then he turned to wait for more of her arguments.

She crossed her arms over her chest, realizing too late she was braless and just pushed her ladies up to the forefront, catching his attention, which was evident by the flash of heat in his eyes.

Refusing to budge, she chose another route. "I don't have any cat food. Or litter boxes."

"They're young yet, so milk will be fine, and I can shred some paper for them."

Dang. He was good.

Sensing another argument, he pushed. "You can compost it."

Smart aleck.

"Well, they need a bath."

"Agreed."

Neither one made a move. Cuddles waited, eyeing them both.

"How did you find them and know the mother was dead?" Maybe he'd tell her, maybe he wouldn't, but at this point he owed her something for barging into her life.

Unease crossed his features as his internal struggle with telling her the truth played through his handsome features. "I can communicate with them."

Spencer couldn't help the laugh that escaped. The look on his face told her he thought she didn't believe him.

"Talking to animals must come in handy in your line of work." Oh, snap. Hope he never talked to Bessy or Tulip, or she'd have a lot of explaining to do.

"At first, until it didn't work anymore. But lately, my gift seems to be working." The thought perturbed him.

"So would he really prefer Apollo?" She inclined her head toward to her loyal German shepherd.

Bennett's lips quirked. "He loves you, so Cuddles from you is okay."

She smiled warmly down at the dog, who lolled his tongue out. "All right. Let's get your little kitty pride cleaned up and smelling fresh before we get them some milk."

***

Back pressed against the wall, Dani bit into Mercury's shoulder to keep from crying out as he pumped into her. They were in the broom closet, for heaven's sake. Pitch black with the door shut, but it hadn't slowed them down when she stripped her pants off and wrapped her legs around her mate, and he slammed into her.

She'd actually been making headway breaking into the phone that Bennett took off the recruit who had attacked his woman. Dante was finally napping in his little bassinet in her office when Mercury tapped lightly on her office window.

The walking dead feeling left her as the fire in Mercury's swirling eyes grew, and they ducked into the closet for some afternoon delight. They never knew how long they had, so opportunities were seized where ever and whenever, and almost always during naptime. Unless Dani was napping herself; Mercury damn near lost an arm if he so much as thought about touching her.

Their simultaneous orgasms done, they clung to each other, chests heaving. Mercury hands roamed over her body, climbing up her shirt.

Untwining her legs, Dani stepped away to hunt for her pants, earning a deep sigh from her frustrated mate.

"Why do you push me away?" He had never asked her that before. She had hoped he'd be okay with their clandestine liaisons that lacked long caresses.

"I need to get back to researching the recruit's contacts in the phone." Dani managed to sound all businesslike, like nothing was wrong.

"Daniella." Mercury's warning tone told her she wasn't leaving the broom closet until she started talking.

"My body's just not bouncing back as fast as I thought it would, especially being mated. I should've healed by now." Her stretch marks were gone, thankfully. She had enough to be insecure about. Dante had been large and it was a tough delivery, one that would have ended with surgery if not for the strength of her mating bond that gave her speedier healing, helping make the birth successful.

But the motherfucking baby weight! Dani struggled with her own care, and Dante kept her more than a little busy. She couldn't shower most mornings, barely functioned out of a zombie state, and couldn't stand to look at herself. And Mercury wanted to touch her all over.

"You're talking crazy, you're beautiful."

"Even you said I should probably wear maternity pants a little longer."

Mercury stilled. He had caught her trying on her premagnum belly yoga pants and proceeded to make a suggestion that she still wear maternity pants if they fit better. Oh yeah, that'd been a hell of fight, one that consisted of her kicking him out and throwing his clothes on the front porch before crying and picking them all up until he directed her to bed and lovingly tucked her in for a nap.

"Daniella, you were near tears. I thought I was making a helpful suggestion that would make you feel better. It was blind stupidity, we covered that."

Dani found her pants and climbed into them. They weren't maternity ones anymore, but she still felt lumpy and bumpy. He really had been trying to help, only seeking to make her mood improve, but his legendary bluntness bit him in the ass.

"Daniella, talk to me." His concern caved her.

"I just don't want you to see me until I get my body back and it's taking forever. I don't want you to change your mind."

"How can you be worried about that?" He sounded truly incredulous. "Honey, I love you tight and athletic. I love you with a large, round belly growing my child. And I love you with a—what did you call it? Muffin top?"

Oh, no he didn't. Before she could plan on how many of his clothes she would throw out on the porch, he continued.

"I've been dying to explore every new inch of you and whether it stays or goes, I don't care. Those new boobs of yours, though, I would really like a shot at them."

She could feel the heat of his gaze on her D-cup milk laden breasts even in the dark room. Her night vision was improving from being mated to a shifter, but his sight was much more acute.

"They're just temporary," she mumbled, worried that once she went back to her B cup, he would lose interest in that part of her anatomy.

"'Sokay. I just want to play with them while they're around. And I'll thoroughly enjoy them if they go back to pert little mouthfuls."

Insecurity crinkled her brow. She wanted to believe him and this was so unlike her. Self-confidence wasn't something she'd ever lacked. A larger than life, exotically gorgeous shifter, who may be one of the only shifters alive who could pick his own mate, made her new mom, sleep deprived hormones go haywire.

His heat crowded around her as he skimmed his hands up and down her arms. "Why don't we try a sitter again?" his voice rumbled in front of her face. "Have a night for just the two of us."

"Typical male, thinking sex can cure anything." Teasing humor laced her voice. A few hours alone with him sounded really nice. "But you know what happened last time."

"Uncle Benji may not be our best sitter option."

A giggle slid past her lips when she remembered how harried the controlling Guardian appeared when they showed up early to pick up Dante, who had already blown out a window and knocked several items off shelves in the shifter's cabin. Twelve pounds of baby versus two-hundred forty pounds of male and it was no contest.

"You think Jace and Cassie would be open to babysitting?" The grounded, mated couple might be willing to help out.

"Maybe they could be the responsible ones and Kaitlyn could entertain." Mercury's idea might actually work. The gregarious redhead adored Dante, but got a little flustered when the fussiness couldn't be calmed down by cooing and rattles.

Three grown adults *should* be able to keep a powerfully gifted baby from demolishing a cabin.

"It would be nice to have sex somewhere other than a janitor's closet," Dani pondered.

"We don't have a janitor, and we do our own cleaning, so it's just a closet." Mercury couldn't help stating the obvious sometimes.

A hesitant chirp signaling that a full-blown wail of impending doom would soon follow, along with her heavy breasts, told her it was feeding time.

She gave Mercury a quick kiss that lingered longer than intended until Dante's cries started bearing more urgency. She led the way out of the closet across the hall from her office of monitors and gadgets.

"Do you have a minute? I have some info from the phone Bennett brought in that you can pass onto Commander Fitzsimmons."

He picked up the squirmy bundle with dark brown hair that gleamed like his daddy's, except golden and not silver, when he was expressing strong emotion. Mercury bobbed and cooed with his son while Dani settled into a chair, preparing to nurse.

"What do you have?" He handed Dante to his mommy, getting lost for a second in the boy's dark brown eyes that gleamed like burnished gold under the office light.

Dani settled in for the feeding, enjoying Mercury's rampant awe at the mother-baby bond. "Well, I haven't tracked any of the outgoing calls yet, but I noticed a pattern of sorts. This guy called the same five or so numbers each night, multiple times. So I'm thinking if he was searching for the unknown woman, he might have been checking in with other recruits."

Mercury nodded thoughtfully. "From what Bennett was told by Christian, it sounds like they were blanketing the area looking for her at clubs and bars. It would make sense they wouldn't want to double up their efforts on bar-hoppers or frequent flyers."

"I'll work on tracing the numbers, but the contacts in the phone are assigned lowercase letters. Do you think they're prospective agents, with wishful thinking of what letter they'd earn after training?"

Sigma attracted demented young men and women recruits looking for a life where violence earned them power. Or in Dani's case, revenge for her family's slaying. Unlike many, she came to realize how twisted and wrong the organization was, and with her mate's help, freed herself and their baby from the evil Madame G's clutches.

Those recruits who found favor with chapter leaders and survived training were elevated to Agent status. Then they were given the weapons and resources to hunt shifters, and sometimes also vampires who didn't buy into Sigma's vision of dominating shifter-kind for their personal use.

How Bennett's mate fit into this grand plan, they weren't sure. The bullshit line fed to the recruits about an alpha hybrid didn't make sense to those who understood how the species reproduced. And according to Bennett, the woman was human.

"No doubt they're hoping to reach Agent status. I'll update the commander and we'll give him the rest when you trace the numbers."

"So, he's staying with her for real, huh?" Dani didn't want to see Bennett hurt. He meant a lot to Mercury and was warming up to Dani, moving beyond friendly to brotherly.

"It's only 'for her protection'." Mercury gave the last words air quotes, amusement lighting his eyes.

"You enjoy watching his demise." Dani did, too. Even though she and Bennett were bonding over their love and respect for her mate, Mercury, the blond could be a major dick and he needed a mate who wouldn't take his shit.

"I do." Mercury turned serious. "But only if it turns out completely opposite of last time." He stopped to consider his partner's situation. "It feels right, though. I haven't officially met her, but he's slowly becoming Benji again."

"He changed that much after Abigail's betrayal?" Dani couldn't imagine Bennett without the debonair attire and perfectly coifed hair.

"No, before. Pretty much right after he met her. She feared who he was so much, even before she found out he was a shifter, that he cleaned himself up and acted differently so as not to scare her. Then, after the rescue when the dust settled, he changed his name and how he dressed and acted."

"What if this Spencer betrays him, too?"

"Then we'll take care of her like we did Abigail."

***

She was going to kill him. The male wouldn't leave, and Spencer was getting desperate. Not from his overtly male pheromones, constantly reminding her of the pleasure he could bring her fully clothed. Or the imaginings of the unclothed ecstasy his large, powerful body promised to deliver.

No, it was from the physical exertion she performed next to him each day for the last three days working her land. Thankfully, he wasn't interested in her lovely cows, thinking they were dear pets she had dragged across the country with her to settle in and start her life.

But three days of toiling in the early summer sun was wearing her down. Even Bennett had noticed and asked if she was okay. She bit his head off and earned a, "Sorry I gave a shit, I mean, sugar, or whatever the hell you say instead of shit," in return.

She needed to visit Bessie or Tulip desperately, or she would attack Bennett. He was damn near irresistible, making her fangs ache with his proximity, but the last few days of manual labor kept him from his normal grooming habits and the results were freaking devastating.

Scruff covered his face, his hair naturally rumpled from his disarming habit of shoving his hands through it, and his clothes…good gawd. Gone were the black sweats he arrived in, and there was no hint of the stylish clothing he usually donned. For planting in her small fields, he was all western shirts and worn blue jeans. The idea of cowboy boots on that male made her swell with rampant desire, it was embarrassing.

They were both swamped by the sensuality emitted by the other. Her only defense was that he assumed she couldn't sense his. It didn't take special senses to feel his hot gaze roam her body as she bent, working in the soil. It certainly didn't take enhanced eyesight to spot the perma-erection he maintained.

Keeping their distance from each other only made them both cranky. Biting comments and grunts of replies were their main source of dialogue, so they were left with trying to avoid each other. Some nights he went out for a run, and she desperately hoped tonight he'd do the same so she could go give Tulip a big ol' hug.

A furry little bundle attacked her left boot. A smile lifted her lips as the one they called Cougar, ferociously batted at her booted toe until a second striped ball of fur, Siber, jumped the first kitty.

"Good sneak attack. I didn't even notice you stalking me." Of course she'd been a little distracted by the sweaty male hauling fallen limbs and branches from the trees to her rented wood chipper.

Homegrown mulch and compost, and free, couldn't beat it.

The kittens trotted off, planning to stalk Cuddles, who with Bennett's help, was quite tolerant of the new additions. Cuddles stuck to sleeping with Spencer in her room, taking up almost all of the space on her worn mattress, while the kittens tucked in around Bennett. It was cute as heck and he had glared bullets at her when she broke out in peals of laughter the first morning she found them all snuggled up together.

"I'm going to fire up the grill and make some dinner."

Bennett nodded his acknowledgement. At this point, she could eat her steak raw, but for now it was rare to medium-rare for the both of them.

She finished cooking dinner, adding grilled asparagus that Bennett scowled at but ate. He carried his meal out to the front porch while she ate in the kitchen, again keeping their distance from each other. The sexual tension between them could be cleaved with their steak knives. Even Cuddles felt the unease, pacing back and forth between them.

Going back out to work to take advantage of every minute of daylight, they cleared, dug, and planted. She owed Bennett, she really did. Not just for his protection, for that she was grateful as things had been heating up in Sigma's hunt for her, but also for his manual labor. She had so much more in the ground at this point, it would increase her production considerably, and give her a heck of a start.

"Spencer, I'm heading out to run." With daylight fading, Bennett circled around back to strip, the thought making her mouth water, and she heard him lope off into the woods.

Finally.

Chapter Seven

That woman made his blood boil. Bennett avoided all of her traps while he let his wolf run. The fresh, clean air filtered through his lungs, the running gait stretched out kinks from the day's work.

After his unexpected release in her truck a few nights ago, he'd experienced the first sense of relaxation. Because the release was thanks to his mate, he could have enjoyed the ease of tension for days. Maybe even weeks. But not when he was stuck here in a living hell of being close to her sexual napalm.

He couldn't take the chance. She might know about their species and mating, but he was sure it'd be a different story if he told her she was his destined mate. He refused to be with another woman if that meant he had to hide his true nature. He might be fine censoring his language around her, only because he enjoyed hearing what she used as cussing substitutes. Otherwise, he was a jackass, liked his space, preferred to be in charge, and if he were to take a mate, which wouldn't happen, he planned to mark the ever-loving shit out of her.

He had held back with Abigail, didn't mark her out of alarm it would be too much for her, and held his nature in check in bed. It was all sweet poetry, declarations of love, and only the missionary position. He had loved his wife, like a male should love his mate. Her gentle innocence offset his rough nature, her tall slender body would have cradled him like a glove if she had ever let herself relax and enjoy sex. He had worked tirelessly to bring her to orgasm and it almost sent her running home to confess her sins to her parents and beg to return.

So if he were to accept another mate, which wouldn't happen, it simply wouldn't be another human female.

Bennett's mind wandered to the conversation he had with Mercury the previous night. Spencer wanted to free her brother, and he suspected she would plan it with or without the Guardian's help. Commander Fitzsimmons felt the focus might be on hunting Spencer, although Sigma certainly monitored young Ronnie Newton. If the Guardians freed him and prevented him from contacting Spencer, they could keep her safe.

Mercury also updated him on what Dani gathered from the recruit's phone. Kaitlyn was sent out to go clubbing with Jace, a task she was more than qualified for, and she spotted two more recruits hunting girls. Eliminating them would only alert Sigma. The Guardians learned more about the mystery woman now, thanks to Jace's special power of influence. The recruits told him as much as they knew about their mission.

Unfortunately, there was still jack shit to go on. They were charged to find a woman in her twenties, who was evasive about her family and new to town. Then they needed to get a blood sample to take back to their compound for testing, hence the wicked rings used to prick the skin. Dani also checked into missing girl cases in the area and found three women had disappeared in the last several months who could have fit the description of the one the recruits were assigned to find.

The missing women were undoubtedly dead. He could tell Spencer, use her guilt to get her to reveal what she was hiding, but he feared it would influence her to go on the run again. Then, not only Spencer, but more women, would suffer.

Bennett pulled up short when he heard Mercury's warning in his head. Dani spotted four Agents, heading toward Spencer's house.

Fuck! Bennett spun, his claws kicked up dirt as he dug in, racing toward the house.

Spencer! Agents!

He flew through the trees, dodging her traps, hoping his mental call worked on his human mate.

Faint sounds of struggle pricked his ears. Mercury and the commander were each taking on an Agent.

His eyes picked out the house through the trees. Every single light was on, inside and out. Smart girl. One of the remaining Agents crouched under the cover of the porch where the light didn't reach. The other Agent was likely hunting near the back door. Bennett sensed Spencer inside, armed with her shotgun and Apollo.

The Agent was so intent on grabbing Spencer, he didn't see the large, light brown wolf until it was too late. Bennett bit down hard on the Agent's carotid until warm, sour blood pumped into his mouth. The Agent flailed as both of them tumbled on the ground. Bennett ground down his jaw, shaking his head, not letting go until the Agent's movements ceased, even after hearing a shotgun blast from inside the house.

Rushing to help, he saw nothing but a peppered Agent stumbling out the back door. Spencer managed to wound him enough that Apollo could attack, but the Agent would probably recover quickly and the dog could get killed.

Stay back, Bennett ordered Spencer, rushing out to aid Apollo in killing the last Agent. Mercury and Commander Fitzsimmons would arrive in seconds. The Agents hadn't been expecting a pack of Guardians when they came for Spencer and were easily taken by surprise.

Apollo was growling, latched onto the last Agent's arm, whose unnatural enhancements allowed him to overcome the shotgun pellets and fight off the dog. A glint of silver alerted Bennett to a gun pointing toward the German shepherd.

Ripping the arm with the weapon away from Apollo, Bennett dove for the neck, latching on. The

Agent grabbed for a knife sheathed on his torso, slicing Bennett's shank, and fuck if that didn't burn. As the Agent's movements stilled, Bennett registered Apollo's absence, along with the maddening woman's.

He called out to Commander Fitzsimmons. *She ran. I need to find her!*

Go! We'll collect the bodies and burn them. And Bennett, bring her in.

That was going to piss her off. She had a major secret, but not for much longer. Next time, Sigma will send more Agents and that shotgun won't be enough.

Sniffing around, Bennett stopped short when he found a pile of clothing—a tank top, worn work jeans, and boots; exactly what Spencer had been wearing. Bennett lifted his nose, sniffing the air.

What. The. Fuck. It couldn't be possible.

Yet…it wasn't unheard of. Kaitlyn's scent wasn't as distinct as other female shifters when they first met her, in fact, it had been downright human. The tall redhead hadn't even known she was a shifter until only a year ago. Oh, but Spencer knew what she was, and why she hid it was the million-dollar question.

Bennett raced through the trees until he spotted a sleek, fine looking brown wolf. White streaks ran through her fur, just like the highlights in her hair, resulting in an ultra-feminine appeal that sang to his wolf. He couldn't slow to admire her canine form, he needed to catch her. She was fast, but only as fast as her companion. Her love for the dog would help Bennett catch her.

Spencer, stop!

Did she just speed up? Dammit!

Deliberately, she ran faster, jumping over her traps in hopes that Bennett would get snagged by one since he was so close behind her. Soon, they would be free of her land and he could pursue her more easily. He could've gotten to her already, but the injury slowed him. In fact, he *shouldn't* have caught her, something was slowing her down as well, other than being unwilling to leave behind Apollo. She'd been looking pale and weak the past few days. Maybe she wasn't feeling well?

With a final surge, he covered the distance between them and sprang onto her back. Trying to attach to the scruff of her neck as they rolled, she knew what he intended to do and transitioned back to her human form.

In a panic, he did too in order to prevent himself from sinking his teeth or claws into her fine, golden skin. He wrestled with her, she was surprisingly strong, even for a female shifter, until he had her pinned under him, wrists clamped in his hand.

Chests heaving, they both took stock of each other. Blood loss, pain, and physical exertion didn't stop his body from reacting to the feel of her smooth, muscular body underneath him.

Spencer's eyes widened as he grew hard against her belly. He could scoot down and still be able to keep her wrists shackled, but that would put his persistent member at ground zero, and her round globes with dusky peaked nipples too close to his mouth.

Apollo whined close to the prone couple, and Bennett sent him a warning look not to interfere. This was between him and his mate. His *shifter* mate.

"Get off me Bennett," she said between clenched teeth.

Oh, but he could smell her desire, see the pinkened cheeks, feel her quickened breaths, all for the naked male on top of her.

"Sure thing, sweetheart."

Yanking her wrists, he pulled her up with him, and slung her over his shoulder, her fine ass right next to his face.

"Wha—Put me down! Bennett!" She struggled, beating at his back, kicking out her legs. "I can walk just fine."

Instinct spurred him to nip her butt, earning him a shriek of disbelief and outrage, and that, along with another spike in her desire made him grin.

"Yeah, and you can run, too. But we need to talk." Stomping through the woods, he carried his furious cargo while Apollo trailed behind.

"Where are we going?" She was compliant now, twisting only to try and look around.

"The commander said to bring you in." Her scent was driving him crazy. His engorged shaft was making walking painful, but at least it diverted blood away from his knife wound so only one part of his body throbbed.

He was covered in blood, so maybe he'd shower before their talk. He planned to talk long and hard with this female.

"I'm not your prisoner!"

"Nope. You're under our protection."

"I don't want it." If he thought she was furious before… "I've done just fine without the Guardians."

"Exactly. Why wouldn't you want the Guardians' help?" It was their duty to protect shifters.

She remained silent and another thought occurred to him.

"Tell me, little shifter. Do you sense I'm your mate?"

She tensed and he had his answer, his anger rose to match her fear.

"And you didn't think you could trust me?" She'd known all this time. It was real, he had another destined mate and she wasn't human. He could be saved.

"I trust no one but my family."

He tromped through the trees, desire burning through him, his destination near. Her family? Other than her crazy brother in the padded room?

His cabin came into view, and he walked straight inside and kicked the door shut behind him.

Her sharp inhale indicated she knew this was his home. "That's right, darlin'," his drawl bled through the words, "you're mine."

Oh, no. No, no, no, no. This was some real bull-pucky she was in. Hanging upside down, seeing nothing but Bennett's toned, taught butt and strong muscular legs, while smelling his blood when she'd been so close to dealing with her weakness...it was overwhelming. The Agents showed up before her task with her cows was completed, and now she was even more deficient than before.

He slid her down his body, slowly, savoring every bare inch of her. Aw, heck, she was in trouble. Setting her on her feet facing him, she swayed slightly. Mistaking her unsteadiness for the revulsion at his bloodied state, he tipped his head down, closer to hers.

"I can shower first," he spoke quietly, his voice dropping a few husky octaves. "But you'd have to join me."

The blood had a sour taint to it but she didn't care. The hard, naked male before her had saved her more than once, she was tired, had been ridden by want for this shifter for days, and now he knew part of her secret. Thankfully, not the most critical part.

Reaching up to grab his head and pull him down to her, he matched her eagerness, lifting her up to him. Their lips smashed together; her tongue seeking to taste, his to dominate.

She wrapped her legs around his waist as they were still standing in his entryway. Grabbing her butt, having smelled her need, and knowing how ready she was, he lifted her and placed her hot, wet entrance at the tip of his shaft. Where he might have hesitated, not wanting to hurt her with his large size, she tightened her legs to draw herself down along his length more quickly.

Growling rattled his chest, he acquiesced and slammed up into her. They both broke their kiss and cried out. Finally, she felt full and it felt right.

Catching deep blue eyes that burned with fiery passion, she rocked her hips while he gripped her butt, setting the pace. His eyes burned into hers as he drove them both quickly to an explosive end.

Her walls quaked around him, and she threw her head back to cry out his name when he dropped his head to where her neck met her shoulder, and his searing tongue licked her.

She feared he intended to mark her. The thought alone was almost too much. Her cry turned into a wail as the intensity of the pleasure ripped through her and he followed, pumping his release within her.

Chest heaving, still tightly wrapped around Bennett in all ways, one thought burned through her haze. *How dare he!*

"You almost claimed me!" She was outraged. She worked so hard to remain hidden and blend into the human world, and this male nearly shattered it all with a little love nip. No matter that it was an amazing thought that sent lightning bolts of ecstasy through her live-wire body.

"Course I did. You're mine." That slight southern drawl of his, the one he hid most of the time, went right through to her core, sending more moisture in preparation of another bout with her mate. "Tell, you what," he drawled through half-lidded eyes, "you can mark me first."

She was about to open her mouth to argue when he thrust inside of her. It. Felt. So. Good. Soon enough, her mouth was busy again with his as he moved them into another room and sat on a bed, his bed. She assumed he'd lay her down and was ashamed at her anticipation of feeling his weight cover her. Instead, he remained sitting on the edge of his bed, lifting her up and down along his shaft until she took over, riding him smoothly, enjoying each stroke and the miniscule control it gave her over the commanding male.

Since he didn't need his hands to set the pace anymore, Bennett put them to good use massaging her breasts with one while finding her center with the other, making her gasp. Holding onto his shoulders, she quickened her pace, the quick circles of his fingers igniting an impending explosion. Her face dropped down into the crook of his neck as she worked his length, the pleasure short-circuiting her good sense, allowing her sense of survival to take over and grab what her body so very much needed.

He presumed she was going to mark him, but she needed so much more. A dark recess in her brain screamed at her to stop, but Bennett changed his rhythm, pushing her over the edge. As she came around him, and he climaxed within her, she opened her mouth wide, allowing her fangs to drop with exhilaration and strike his vein.

Strength surged within her as his blood pumped into her mouth. Swallowing greedy mouthfuls, she was unprepared for the power contained in a shifter's blood, much less a shifter as virile as a Guardian.

Healing whipped through her blood after being deprived for so many days of sunny manual labor. Combined with the electric surge of Bennett's power, Spencer couldn't help but let the blackness claim her.

Chapter Eight

Frozen underneath the gorgeous, supple, apparently unconscious body of his mate, Bennett's mind started functioning again. Then almost quit, refusing to acknowledge his mate's secret. Couldn't be.

No fucking way.

It was the ultimate paranormal urban legend.

Yeah, just like finding two mates in one lifetime was shifter myth.

Fuck me.

Bennett carefully lifted his little shifter—scratch that—*hybrid* off his lap. He tried not to groan and become hard again when he slid out of her, at the same time her fangs disengaged from his neck, sending a jolt of awareness that those little fangs were lethal in bed. And shifters thought the mating bite enhanced pleasure. It had nothing on the vampire's bite. When her bite sunk through his skin, he'd been blinded by the explosion of pure ecstasy.

No wonder they could seduce their food supply so easily.

Bennett's eyes narrowed as he covered Spencer's still form with a blanket. How did she feed?

He took his time searching her face, admiring the dark blonde eyelashes that were swept down onto her cheeks, a sign she was resting peacefully, even snoring gently. Hell, that was cute. He was in so much trouble.

Going to the front door and opening it, he eyeballed the dark, furry shape sitting on his porch.

How does she feed?

Images of grilling and prepping vegetables for dinner filled Bennett's head.

Blood, Apollo.

Apollo whined and craned his neck to peek into the cabin, checking on his companion. Catching the scent of intimacy, Apollo finally caved, and Bennett clearly saw Bessie and Tulip in his mind. Relief swamped him and what a hypocrite. He was what Dani had called Mercury when she first met him, a manwhore. Yet, he was worried that Spencer was out trolling for guys to bite during sex to supply blood.

Cows? What a clever little hybrid. "I saved them as calves. They're like family," my ass. Bennett snorted remembering when he asked why she would have two cows that weren't even good for milking.

Bennett wandered back inside and meandered all over his bedroom, dragging his hands through his hair several times, trying to figure out how to proceed. Finally, he cast out a message to the commander and Mercury. They should be done with dead Agent burning detail by now.

Throwing on a pair of shorts and grabbing a handled woven basket Kaitlyn had bought him because it was, "sixty-percent off, and it was, like, two bucks!" he then headed out to wait on the porch. Setting the basket down, he gave Apollo some instructions. The dog grabbed the basket and loped off.

So he was worried about the kittens. He wasn't a complete bastard.

"No way." Mercury, in complete disbelief, approached the steps.

Bennett clenched his jaw, seriously dreading this conversation.

Commander Fitzsimmons propped a boot up on the first step. "So you weren't cursed with another human mate?"

"Definitely not human," Bennett said grimly.

Mercury trotted up the steps. "Kaitlyn smelled human because she hadn't shifted, probably since puberty, and we thought her parentage involved an ancient."

Bennett nodded thoughtfully. When they found out Kaitlyn was shifter living a completely human life, he thought she reminded him of an ancient he had encountered decades ago. Now they were wondering if it wasn't from lack of shifting. Or both.

The commander's brow furrowed. "Has Spencer not shifted for years?"

Bennett shrugged, the movement catching Mercury's attention. The massive male next to him went still.

"Duuuuude, are those fangs marks?" Mercury leaned even closer, making Bennett want to hide them and forget about telling those closest to him his mate's deepest secret. The commander stood straighter, his face deadly serious.

Biting the bullet, he went for it. "She's a hybrid."

Mercury stated the obvious. "Shiiiit."

***

Why wasn't she waking up?

It was morning and Bennett dozed on and off in the uncomfortable chair in his bedroom, unwilling to crawl into bed with another mate, unwilling to go there emotionally. Kinda like why he never planned on having sex in the missionary position again.

The commander decided to table further speculation on the hybrid until Spencer actually provided answers, and they could determine if she was lying or not. In the meantime, they'd warn the others living in and around the lodge to be on heightened alert.

Finally, Bennett's attention was brought to the rustling of covers and Spencer stretching her arms above her head. The image of breasts almost popping out the top of the blanket and her noises of contentment immediately sent heat to his groin. *Bad time, buddy.*

Spencer sat up, holding the blanket to her chest, and glanced around like she'd never seen the place. Well, guess she didn't get the full tour last night. When she looked questioningly at Bennett, color slowly leeched from her face as she read his solemn expression.

"I have some clothes you can put on before we go talk to my team." A tick worked in his jaw when fear claimed her features. "We can help you."

"It's not just me I'm trying to protect," she whispered, tears springing up in her eyes.

Aw, hell. He hated tears in a woman. They made him feel like a monster.

"Get dressed," he said abruptly.

Tears ran down her face and her hands shook as she grabbed the shirt and shorts he laid on the end table for her. "Uh, the bathroom?"

"You can get dressed out here. I don't want to chase you again." Liar. He'd love to chase her. Her wolf was beautiful, and those little fangs…

Spencer sighed and maneuvered her legs into the shorts and covered herself with the shirt without baring another inch of skin, much to his disappointment.

His clothes were extremely large on her, and he couldn't do anything about her bare feet, so he stormed out of his cabin heading toward the lodge, expecting her to follow.

When they passed Apollo, with the kittens nestled into the dog's warm fur, Bennett ordered him to remain by the cabin. Spencer followed quietly, wiping her tears, attempting to regain her composure. He waited for her to use her tears to change his mind about forcing her to talk to his team, but she didn't. He should be surprised, but his mate had never acted like he expected. And he always expected the worst from a female.

Bennett strode into the lodge, making his way toward the interrogation room.

A shadow moved out of the hallway. The white-haired, baby blue-eyed Parrish peered beyond Bennett to Spencer. Bennett drew to a halt, waiting to see what the youth intended. Parrish rarely ventured out of the basement away from his gaming systems, and all the Guardians were worried about how he would do with Master Bellamy's impending intervention.

Spencer hovered behind Bennett, unsure of the peculiar, young male shifter.

Parrish's hands moved in a flurry, Bennett tried to keep up.

"What do you mean she's not the one they're looking for?" Bennett spoke, forgetting to simultaneously sign back, not that the kid needed it since his hearing was just fine. Spencer tensed behind him, and he feared she really would try to run.

Parrish waved his hand back and forth, indicating Bennett had it wrong. Pausing for a second, he signed more slowly, considering his words more carefully and making sure Bennett fully understood.

"She's the one they are looking for, but the wrong one. They are after the wrong one." Bennett let that sink in, Spencer held her breath behind him. Her confusion rolled off her in waves. He knew the feeling.

"Sigma's after a hybrid and they think it's her, but it's not?"

Parrish nodded emphatically.

"Then who?" Bennett couldn't believe it. More hybrid women?

Purity, was all Parrish signed before literally running off. That boy needed a good interrogation himself. He needed to start spilling what he knew and how, and quit being treated like a fragile head case.

"What was that last part he signed?" Spencer asked.

Falling back on being an asshole, Bennett said, "He said you weren't pure."

Anger permeated the air. "Well, not after last night." Her prim declaration carried a hint of derision, managing to completely insult him.

An involuntary chuckle escaped him. "Come on, they're waiting."

An interrogation room? Oh no he didn't.

"What is this, Bennett?" She stopped with her hands on her hips, not entering the room. Two large men waited in the room, and she scented two more individuals, a human female and another shifter, close by.

"This is Commander Fitzsimmons." He gestured to the tall, ruddy-haired male already sitting at the table, and then to the hulk leaning against the wall with his arms crossed, examining her speculatively, "This is my partner, Mercury. We need to talk with you."

"Then why does the room say 'interrogation' next to it if we're just going to *talk*? And who's in the next room?" She was demanding some of her own answers if these Guardians expected her to roll over on her whole family.

Sadly, she might need to do just that. Sigma would keep amping up their attacks. She was good, but there was little chance she could have escaped four Agents, and not without serious injury and probably getting Apollo killed.

"It's the best place to conduct an interview, private and secure. Our security expert is in the next room to record and gather data."

Panic welled up. A recording had too much potential to fall into the wrong hands, no matter how many security measures were taken. "Oh, no. No recording, or I'm not talking."

"Spencer, we're only here to help you." The gentle, placating tone in his voice irritated her.

"Don't you dare think you can sweet talk me with your massive charm, Mr. Young. I've been running almost half my life, and I'm not still alive because I'm gullible or stupid. Give me your word I will not be recorded or I'm not talking." Hands still on her hips, she even started tapping her foot, refusing to quit glaring into Bennett's navy blues even after she heard the one called Mercury snort and try to cover it up with a cough.

The commander narrowed his eyes on her and mulled over her words. "It's all right Bennett."

"Fine, Spencer. You have my word, now go on and have a seat."

"Age before beauty," she said sweetly, gesturing for him to move out of her way.

"Holy shit, Benji," Mercury exclaimed. "She's nothing like Abigail."

Benji? Now, that wasn't a name she thought fit him, but it worked with the rugged Bennett with the facial scruff and worn work clothes.

"Abigail?" Spencer cocked her eyebrow at the glowering male, giving Mercury a WTF look.

Ripping his eyes away from his partner, Bennett pinned her with a challenging look. "My wife."

"Ah." So that was her name. "Where you mated or just married?"

The commander cleared his throat. "Bennett can fill you in on his personal history after you tell us about yourself."

Gosh, that male was dour. He was ruggedly handsome with his short reddish-blond hair and serious hazel eyes, but one could tell immediately he wasn't a jovial being, full of mirth. It was like the weight of the world rested on his broad shoulders, and he was ready to kick butt and take names.

Bennett sat across from her, next to his commander. She glanced back at the massive male behind her. He wasn't as tall as Bennett, but was built like a brick outhouse. Although his eyes and hair were black, silver gleamed through them. No wonder they called him Mercury.

"So the human in the next room is your mate?" she asked. Now that she was closer, she could sense way more than the tie between the two.

Mercury's gaze flicked to the two-way glass and warmed with affection. "She is."

"Oh. Congratulations on the little one."

Surprise that she sensed the baby also flared through Mercury's eyes, but he sensed the honesty in her words and nodded his thanks.

"Why do you smell like a human when you're a hybrid, Spencer?" The commander was done with small talk.

"I am human." The males remained still. "My mom's human, my dad's a true hybrid. Our theory is that one species is dominant at a time."

"But you drink blood and change into a wolf," Bennett pointed out.

"Right. I rarely change, because we've found that increases the shifter scent I give off."

The males' gazes flitted around to each other. "That would explain why Kaitlyn passed off as human for so long," Bennett muttered. "What about the vampire part of you?"

"We figured that with the other two species, I don't have all of the vampire urges. I need a small maintenance dose of blood, and bovine blood has proven adequate. If I'm in the sun a lot, then I need more blood, because I am still part vampire and the sun will do more damage to me."

"So you choose a profession that consists primarily of working in the sunlight?" Mercury sounded like he couldn't decide if she was incredibly dumb or incredibly clever.

She shrugged. "We learned to live off the land, and it will provide an income while I can remain relatively isolated."

"Tell us about your grandparents. How did they conceive your dad?" This question from the commander.

She resisted the urge to go into the birds and bees story. Something told her this shifter would not find the humor.

"They were a real couple in love. Mated naturally and all. My shifter grandpa was my vampire grandma's true mate and she was his shifter mate. They hid themselves from both species when they fell in love, each worried the other would be destroyed. When my dad was conceived, they were too afraid to confide in anyone. Afraid either government would take my dad and study him."

"Did they have any more kids?"

Spencer thought for a bit. It felt weird to talk about her family at all, after living in secrecy her whole life. The sad fact was that her grandparents and aunt couldn't be hurt anymore.

"One, my aunt. She was quite a bit younger than my dad. Sigma killed her and my grandparents. She was only eighteen. It happened when I was twelve." Her voice almost cracked. The pain was still there, finding out her beloved grandma and grandpa, and her vivacious Aunt Alli were gone, slaughtered beyond recognition. "We had lived in secrecy until then, but after that, we went on the run."

"Do you know why they were killed?" The commander didn't overwhelm her with questions. There was a hint of compassion in his voice.

Nodding, Spencer's guilt welled up. "Because of me. My parents managed to capture one of the Agents hunting us and interrogated her." Spencer's lips curled into a shaky smile despite the morbid topic. "My mom really liked Aunt Alli and showed no mercy. She managed to extract the few details the Agent knew—they were after a young female hybrid." Her family was destroyed because of Spencer. It was a lot of responsibility to grow up under.

"Why not your aunt?"

"It's weird. They didn't realize we were related. My dad's got my grandma's fair features, while my aunt got her looks from my grandpa. Their information just told them that my grandparents would lead them to me, and Aunt Alli was collateral damage. They think my dad was a full shifter and had me with a vampire before he met my mother." Spencer fiddled with her fingers. No tears welled up after all these years, but the topic was still devastating. "They beheaded Grandma, who smelled like a shifter since she only fed off Grandpa. Then they burned them all."

"Where are your parents now?"

"Dunno." At the disbelieving look, she continued, "My parents trained me and Ronnie, and when we each turned eighteen, they gave us money and false documents, and we went our separate ways. I check in periodically with a burner phone."

"Ronnie?" Bennett asked. "Is that his real name? And what's your real name?"

"My name is real, to throw people off. They expect me to be a guy. Yes, Ronnie must've have kept his first name and changed his last, to draw attention to him instead of me by making it look like he was hiding. He's younger than me, so he's lived most of his life trying to protect me." All her family at risk because she dared to be born. No kid should have to go through that.

"Sigma's story is bullshit, Ronnie was right." Bennett turned to his commander. "I mean look at her. She's not going to bring down both species. No offense, Spencer." She waved it off, totally agreeing with him. "Sure she can blend with humans, has some of our strengths, but as far as a dominant new paranormal species? Nah."

The commander rubbed his neck thoughtfully. "She might represent a threat to both vampire and shifter councils. A hybrid species that neither can completely control and might even make them have to cooperate, I could see if one of those entities wanted her dead."

Spencer's stomach bottomed out. She was in more danger than she thought.

"But," he continued, "many of us would be boosted by the widening mating pool and the chance to decrease the war between vampires and shifters. Much of the younger generation of both species wish to live in peace."

"So," Mercury posed the question, "why would Sigma want her dead?"

All three males turned their heads back to her.

"Parrish said it was her they were looking for, but they had the wrong girl. Spencer's not pure enough."

"The fuck you say?" Mercury's words tilted the corner of her mouth. These males had some foul language, but she was warming to them rapidly.

"We've been on this planet for millennia. Shifters have been mating humans for centuries. Vampires haven't mated with different species…that we know of, but it wouldn't be a terrible stretch to assume there are more hybrids than just Spencer and her family." The commander said it so matter-of-factly, not much must ruffle his feathers. "We need to have a long talk with Parrish. He must be referring to her human blood."

"You threaten somebody." Bennett directed his statement to her.

"Besides you?" She was poking the bear, but he couldn't do what he did to her body last night and then treat her like a suspect this morning. And she was hungry, darn it!

"A few more questions and then we'll eat." Commander Fitzsimmons heard her stomach growl, too.

She was embarrassed, but she was starving for real food now since her blood hunger was cured last night. "All right. Let's finish up then. I'm famished and I've got a lot of planting to get in."

"You can't go back to your house, Spencer."

"Sigma only thinks it's the Guardians who keep intercepting their Agents. But it doesn't matter, I need to get the planting done today. The next few days are going to be dreary and rainy, then I'll need to tend to my mushrooms."

"It's too dangerous," Bennett said it with a tone of finality.

"It is dangerous," she agreed, "but I'm not running and hiding anymore. That's not a life. Bennett, I appreciate your help, but I can see your past leaves you fearing a future with me. If you can't commit completely, we're done. I don't want to mate you until your heart's in it." Not true, she'd love to have his body at her disposal. But she'd want more and there was the rub.

"That's not true." Everyone in the room raised an eyebrow at Bennett. "Mostly. Fuck. It's still new and a shock, and yeah, mating hasn't been a good experience for me. There's been three attempts on your life since we met, so we need to focus on that first and find out the real reason why they want you."

"Fine. I need to protect my livelihood. I sunk my money into that land and only have enough to get by on for so long."

"Fine." Bennett echoed her word, but threw in more attitude. "Then you'll stay at my place, and I'll help you during the day."

Her belly heated at the thought, and wasn't that inconvenient. Sitting in a room, getting hot and bothered over having sleepovers with Bennett, and all three males in the room would notice.

"Before we start searching for answers, there's one more issue we need to take care of." The ominous tone of the commander didn't bode well. "Your brother."

Spencer frowned. "What about him? I'd love to get him out, but he's safe in the psych ward, right?" At least until she could figure out how to talk to him without getting each of them killed.

"You'd leave your brother there?" Mercury sounded incredulous.

"Of course I don't want him there, but I'd rather have him safe while we're figuring this out. The key to our hiding is to not know where each other is, so it can't be used against any of us. It's safer for him to not know I'm living here, too." Her brows furrowed. How did they end up in the same area? "Plus, you don't know Ronnie. If he didn't want to be there, he wouldn't be."

The commander pinned her with a hard look. "Yet, now he's at a disadvantage. He thinks he's staying in there to protect you. Sigma knows exactly where he's at and how to get to him." He paused to let those words sink in, but she still didn't understand. Sigma already knew Ronnie was in there. "Your brother doesn't know you're here, right?"

Oh snap! Spencer sucked in a breath. "They could use him against me! And he'd just sit and wait until they abducted him, thinking there was no way they could use him to find me." But they could use him to get to her. She'd jump into Sigma's arms in a heartbeat if it would save her brother. He'd already gone through enough for her.

Bennett cut his hand through his hair, the ruffled style no longer so manicured. "Looks like we need to bust out Ronnie Newton."

Chapter Nine

"**W**hat'd you *mean* she's living in West Creek?" Ronnie Newton, a.k.a. Ronnie King, spewed in disbelief. He was in the same gunmetal gray scrubs as their last visit, his hair sticking up in several directions.

"Hell of a coincidence, now let's go." Jace's voice was strained. After they achieved access to Ronnie several months ago, security had gotten tighter. Thankfully, Jace's powers had gotten stronger, but influencing his way past administration and the nurses had been taxing, and they still had the hardest part coming up.

"I'm mean, I knew she was close, but not actually living here. How did Sigma find her?"

"Not the time Ronnie. We need to go." Bennett was dressed in black slacks and a white lab coat in an attempt to make Jace's persuasions easier to buy.

Jace himself was dressed in scrubs, but both Guardians were strapped down with various weapons under their clothing. Surely recruits, or Agents, surveilled Ronnie and the hospital, especially after their last visit.

"Oh look! She drank from you." Ronnie squinted at Bennett's neck. "No wonder she was drawn to the area. I mean, the voices said you'd be the one who could find her, but I didn't realize…"

"What voices?" Oh great. The last time they talked, Bennett could've sworn the young male was putting on a show, but hearing voices set him firmly on the crazy train. "Never mind, we'll talk later. Let's go."

Gesturing to Jace to lead the way, using his voice and pale eyes to circumvent any trouble, the three males made it all the way to the ground floor, heading toward a lesser used exit closer to where Mercury sat in the Denali.

A burly security guard and a male in a suit came out of a side hallway, blocking their exit.

"This is gonna be good," Ronnie clapped his hands together and giggled. The kid was insane.

Jace spoke, his voice developed a vibrating timbre. "You need to move and let us keep going."

The men stayed where they were, the three males aimed for the door. Bennett's mind calculated how long it would take to neutralize the threat (only seconds), where the security camera feed went so they could tamper with it, and how many other Sigma plants were in the hospital when Ronnie stopped short. Bennett pulled up behind him, Jace halted as well, waiting to take on the two men.

Ronnie held up his hands. "Guys, allow me." He moved his hands around in a flurry, he fingers waggling, drawing the attention of the guard and the suit. They frowned, tensing, waiting for Ronnie to run. "Guess how many fingers I'm holding up?"

Ronnie whipped each hand up in the air, fingers spread. The men didn't move. At all. Almost like they were statues.

"What the fuck?" Jace's deep voice spoke the words running through Bennett's head.

"It's my thing." Ronnie shrugged and shoved his hands in his pockets. "We'd better get going, yo. We've only got another minute or two."

Circling around the frozen men, they exited into the sunshine. They had talked with Spencer only that morning. The commander agreed to help Spencer in her garden so Jace and Bennett could snatch Ronnie in broad daylight, hopefully before Sigma set their sights on him after another failed attempt at grabbing his sister.

Loading Ronnie into the SUV, Bennett remembered that Spencer had said he could leave the hospital when he wanted to. What a handy talent, freezing people. Handier than talking to animals, Bennett thought bitterly. Although talking to animals was pretty damn handy back when horses were the main mode of transport. The mighty creatures weren't too willing to have a creature that smelled like wolf hopping onto their backs. Bennett had been crucial to the team just for his talent back then.

After Abigail had almost destroyed them, until cars had become more prevalent, Bennett worked hard to assure his team didn't make a mistake by saving him. He became second in command after his talent was no longer in as much demand and dedicated his days to the safety of his species. It was working fine until darkness crowded his mind, refusing to be driven away by fighting or sex.

He hadn't thought about the darkness since the night he had Spencer in his arms in her truck. It hadn't bothered him since she was in his life on a daily basis. Hell, even that one orgasm that wasn't even inside her tight, willing body would've held him over for months, just because it was from her. It would've held him over, if he hadn't spent each day and night with her, but even during those days in a haze of lust, the darkness hadn't bothered him. Her scent called to him, her oppositional attitude made him want to kiss her into compliance. Her ass bent over while planting made him yearn to strip her down and make her his in every way possible. She was under his skin and he didn't want to face it.

"It's not your fault." Ronnie spoke up from the back where he sat with Jace. If the kid tried to run, or jump, or attack, they'd stop him.

"Who the fuck are you talking to?" Jace grumbled.

"Benji." Bennett tensed as his old nickname came out of Ronnie's mouth. "The voice in my head said Abigail wasn't your fault. The Sweet Mother thought you needed gentleness and innocence for balance. She was right, but she will not be wrong again."

Bennett's breath stalled like he was suffocating. *Focus on the mission and ignore the ravings of a madman*, became his mantra.

"Voices?" Mercury grunted. "You really crazy?"

"Nope," Ronnie said, his face pressed up to the window. "The voices are real, they aren't mine, and they guide me."

"And they're from who?" Jace asked.

Ronnie swiveled his head to gaze at the shaved-head Guardian. "Dunno. One's a woman. She's been in my head all my life. The other's a dude, on the young side. His voice is pretty recent."

"Do they give you real-time advice, or is it random FYI for you to file away?" Mercury eyeballed Ronnie in the mirror, fascinated with the young male—another shifter that said random shit.

"Whatever they feel like." Ronnie was back to staring at the passing scenery. Poor bastard had been in a padded room for months, no wonder he was like a puppy wanting to hang his head out of the window.

"What other talents do you have?" Jace asked. Bennett was glad the other Guardian was on top of it, asking pertinent questions and getting answers that would either save them or prevent them from being destroyed. "Cuz that freezing people is some cool shit."

"Thanks," Ronnie said absently. "Just that. And my voices."

Great. Voices.

***

Agent X pulled down the barely there skirt of her dress. At least she didn't have to find her panties. Her mission tonight had called for going commando. As Demetrius, one of the vampire leaders of Sigma's Freemont chapter, zipped his pants, she leaned back against the tiled wall of the club's private bathroom and crossed her arms. Her center still thrummed from Demetrius' pounding, and she needed to give the bite marks on her neck time to heal before walking out in public.

"Your information was lacking," she informed the tall vampire, who gave her a smug smirk.

"Now love, do we need to barter for more thorough information?" He bared his fangs and eyed her long, bare legs sticking out of the dress.

There were worse ways to get information regarding her personal vendetta, and worse people to bang while getting it. Although she and Demetrius had settled into a friends with benefits type scenario, she would've preferred just friends. She would've preferred not to have to use her body with any male other than her mate. She would've preferred not to have had her family slaughtered and become enslaved by a mad woman leading an evil organization. But alas, life sucked.

"Hey, I held up my end of the deal. Quite well I might add." His gaze heated at her words. Gah, the guy was a horny bastard. "You plan to let me down? Or do I have to spread the word you finish early?"

Demetrius threw his head back and laughed. They both knew she would be utterly lying and he was hawt with his shoulder length amber hair and pale green eyes, the girls would line up waiting to take their chances.

"X, I hope you don't get yourself killed. I'd miss that sass." His eyes crinkled with mirth and there was that wistful moment she often felt in his company—the one that showed her what life outside Sigma could be like, where she could actually have trusted friends she joked around with.

Her life fucking sucked. But she had a job to do. Right now, the best thing she could do for a friend was get them as far away from Sigma as possible. It worked for Dani, a former recruit; a gentle mental suggestion and Dani ran right to Guardians. Good girl.

"Spill it, vampire. You said you suspected how Madame G gets her inside information? Some kind of seer?"

"Ah, yes. I'm afraid I don't have much more than that. I thought it would be enough for one of our…meetings." He flashed a sexy pout and that irked her. Having sex with him might give her some level of protection within the organization, but it didn't mean she was looking for reasons to drop her pants.

"Demetrius, I hope your true mate is a virgin."

Completely aghast, his chiseled face paled. "*Agent X*, why would you say such a thing? I thought we were *friends*."

She smiled cruelly because that was just fun. Not much could get under the lothario's collar, but vampires were solidly bound to their true mate. There was no stepping outside that union, even after just meeting their treasured eternal partner. The thought of a shy, virginal bride needing gentle persuasion to be bedded with the promiscuous male was satisfyingly hilarious.

Tapping her thigh-high stiletto booted foot with impatience, she needed to get back and talk to her partner, Agent E, or Biggie as she called him. "We assumed Madame G was getting some sort of prophecy or visions, but whether it from was a person or crystal ball, *that* part we don't know. Seriously buddy, if you don't know who, when, or where, it does us no good."

Taking a deep breath to shove the thought of dealing with virgins out of his mind, he turned serious. "I went up to her lair and before I got off the elevator, I thought I heard women talking. One was the madam and the other one sounded scared. Scared, but firm. I heard the unknown woman say, 'the girl from my vision is near, I promise you.'

Yet, when the door opened, it appeared as if Madame G was alone. But love, I will give you this free of charge."

X stopped her foot tapping, intent on Demetrius' words.

"I smelled shifter."

Interesting. "Recognize her?"

"No, but I need to investigate. I suspect Madame G has her own goals that soon won't match up to Sigma's ultimate goal."

"Wiping out shifters, or making us your own personal blood slaves?"

Demetrius shrugged. "Yeah, pretty much," he said cavalierly. There it was, the reason why she chose the big vampire to play these information games with. She suspected that much like her, he had his own agenda, and it was not to the benefit of the Sigma organization.

"Hmmm. She's been sending Agents and recruits out to find a female she thinks is a vampire-shifter hybrid. We've lost them all." Not that it bothered X, good riddance. There weren't many at Sigma she hated to see die, and die they would. Madame G used to take her time and groom her recruits before they reached Agent status. Now, she was giving them physical enhancements and kicking them out into the field before they were ready.

Again, totally fine with X. The main problem was that soon Madame G would send her two best Agents, Agent X and Agent E, after the girl. That couldn't happen. It would jeopardize everything X had worked for the past twelve years.

Demetrius' snort interrupted her musings. "A vampire-shifter hybrid. Like that would ever happen."

Yeah, right.

"It's not so much whether or not a hybrid is possible, but why the girl would pose a threat to Sigma. Madame G wants her dead, not studied."

"That's my confusion also," Demetrius interjected. "Sigma would want to study a hybrid. The councils of each species would fight over her. So why kill her?"

Sigma would want not just her, but her brother as well as the parents, but if Demetrius didn't know about the rest of the family, X certainly wasn't going to mention it. She trusted Demetrius as long as their individual agendas aligned. As far as she knew, Madame G monitored the brother in a psych ward, and as long as he was safe, X stayed as far away as possible.

"Well, enough talk." The big male tidied his hair in the bathroom mirror. "There's lonely women out there I must attend to. Until I have more news…" With a wink and flash of fang, he was gone, leaving her alone in the private bathroom.

She could gussy up her short hair, too. But the just-been-fucked look was prevalent in this establishment and that worked for her. X didn't need a mirror to tell her she was well and truly screwed.

***

Agent E finished strapping his weapons to his body. X needed him before he left for town, but the drive to get where he wanted to be was riding him hard tonight. And didn't that just suck. To go where he most wanted to be, and see the number one thing he didn't want to see. Scratch that. It could be worse and he knew it.

I am Julio Esposito. I'm a cop. My wife's name is Ana Esposito; my son's name is Julio Junior. E silently recited the three sentences that kept him sane and kept his head in the game. Pretty soon, he'd have to alter his statement seeing as his wife, who assumed she was widowed, was engaged to some smooth talking, suit-wearing bastard.

The door to his room swung open as his partner, Agent X sauntered in shimmying her shoulders, singing, "Biggie, Biggie, Biggie, can't you see, sometimes your words just hypnotize me?" Playing off his E designation and the Notorious B.I.G. song, she'd called him Biggie since they first met almost ten years ago.

Damn, if that crazy bitch didn't keep him sane. Not a day went by that he wasn't grateful he and X found each other. He owed her as much as she owed him. After Madame G made him dead to the world and he survived her enhancements, he had found himself thrown in a room with a young X.

He was supposed to use her body that day, part of the mental breakdown in Madame G's training program. But he wasn't that guy, no matter who Madame G threw at him. He did what he had to do with the willing ones, since his previous was life over. Ana thought him dead and it was better for her, and the son he never met, that he stayed that way.

Instead, the day he had been thrown in a room with her, X turned on him and whaddya know? She had a hell of a secret. So he took her under his wing, and they worked so damn well together, they'd stayed partners.

"About time you got here," E grunted, then her scent tickled his nose. "You smell like a fangbanger."

X slammed the door, giving anyone in the hallway a show. It worked well, the little performance they always put on—she came back smelling like another male and he stormed off.

"Uh, probably cuz I got banged by some fangs." She sauntered over to the lone closet in his room where she stored some of her clothes and dug out sweats to throw on over the napkin she called a dress.

Turning serious, he spoke quietly, "You don't have to throw everything away for this mission, X."

"It was thrown away a long time ago, Biggie. And we need the intel."

Same disagreement, different day. He was such a hypocrite. He did the same thing with his body, as long as it meant keeping Sigma thinking he was a loyal Agent who played by most of the rules. Mates, spouses, and happily-ever-afters weren't in the cards for him and his partner, and they would make Sigma pay for taking all of that away.

"Have a drink. I've got to get going."

"She's getting desperate and might send us after the hybrid." X slid off her knee-high boots and climbed into the pajamas.

Sliding up his sleeve and removing the watch he wore on his left wrist, he sat on the bed and she settled down next to him. He'd been thinking Madame G had been growing erratic.

"Won't that be a goat fuck?" he asked rhetorically, lifting his wrist for her.

X's fangs sunk in only as deeply as necessary. Each time, he recalled his shock a decade ago when he got thrown into a room with a broken shifter female only to have his neck almost ripped off by her. He would always protect her and her secret, to the grave if he had to. This little tap into his vein was nothing compared to that first time. If he hadn't been enhanced with healing abilities, he would've been six feet under. Now, her little feedings were a multi-purpose event. It left his scent on her and likewise for him, giving the impression they got it on and that made Madame G happy, because as long as he wasn't having sex with his wife, she was pleased. As long as X was using her body, Madame G's perverse sense of power was secure.

"Did you get anything useful out of the arrogant bastard?" E asked, ignoring the furls of desire her suckling created in him. It came automatically with the feeding and though X was gorgeous, it wasn't her he wanted. Even if they had to sleep with each other, other than when she stayed overnight to keep up the ruse, it wouldn't be the end of the world. But them not having had sex together was a personal coup, a big fuck you to Madame G.

Withdrawing her fangs, she tossed him a little shrug and told him what Demetrius had heard in the elevator. Interesting.

"Go." She shooed him away with her hands. "Go get your creep on." X knew where he went and what he did, why he couldn't leave his old life completely behind. She always covered for him.

"I'll make my exit good."

Yawning, she waved at him to go and sank under the covers of the bed.

E opened the door and growled loudly, "Get his stink off you before I get back," and slammed the door behind him as he left.

Chapter Ten

The delight on Spencer and her brother's face at being reunited was touching, if you were into that shit. Bennett couldn't envision Spencer running up to *him*, arms wide open, smiling big like she did for her brother. Instead, she scowled at Bennett, reminded him to mind his language, and barked orders around her little farm.

The sex he had with his mate over a week ago didn't take the edge off his libido any more than their little tryst in the pickup. He was achy from a body full of desire, cranky from seeing her acting sweet as pie to everyone else but surly with him, and livid at her insistence to keep her farm going. Her life was in danger and she insisted on working out in the open. In the sun no less.

And didn't that just sting his ego. Her little one quarter vampire body labored away out in the sun, and instead of seeking his supple flesh for sustenance, Spencer tapped into both Bessie and Tulip last week.

He let her have the cabin while he showered in the lodge's gym and played Xbox all night with Parrish and Ronnie. The two had bonded quickly over their love of video games and reality television.

Arriving at the cabin each morning to check on his mate, he was greeted with the giant German shepherd, draped across his bed with kittens all over his pillow, and a cheerful Spencer heading out for a day of work. Damn woman.

This morning proved no different. He didn't even have time to shower and shave, much less style his hair before grabbing a fresh pair of work clothes and chasing after her.

Trotting through the shade of the trees, he caught up to her more slowly than he had planned, wanting to watch her jean-clad bottom sway over the uneven terrain. Even the loose t-shirt couldn't hide her curves, and her swept-up hair, tucked under her straw hat, bared her elegant neck, making him remember how he had buried his face there not too long ago.

He was hard again. Fuck!

"Spencer." He trotted to move in front of her so she'd be forced to stop and confront him. "What the hell is your problem with me?"

Her sparkling hazel eyes changed from questioning to mulish in less than a heartbeat.

"Bennett, the fact that you can't figure that out plucks my hide." She rested the ever-present shotgun against the ground and put her other hand on her hip.

"I'm a guy! Of course I don't know why I piss you off. I can speak into minds, but I can't read them. Is it my past with other women?"

Shaking her head, she looked like she almost took pity on him. "No, not the way you think. I'm a shifter, too. I understand our lifestyle. I think it's only one woman in your past that's making you act like such an ass to me."

"Sweet Mother Earth. Did Spencer King just swear?"

"Don't try to dodge the topic. And no, I called you a donkey—a stubborn animal that works hard but doesn't trust easily."

Well, that was highly accurate, and yes, he was trying to dodge the topic. "Yes, Abigail ruined me. She was innocent, fearful—especially of me. I did everything I could to earn her trust, even changed who I was. It wasn't enough."

"That's too bad. I think I would've liked the old Bennett."

"The old Bennett went by Benji, or Benjamin. He was too naïve for his own good, rarely shaved, and wore dirty, dusty clothes."

"You mean like you've been doing these last couple of weeks helping me?"

Bennett paused considering her words. He had been more like his old self working in the dirt all day next to Spencer and she didn't seem to mind.

"You look amazing all dappered out in your GQ clothes. You look hot as heck in your work clothes. And I prefer your hair after you've run your hands through it ten times. No, Bennett, I'm upset because you drag me to your cabin, we have sex, you find out exactly what I am, then you treat me like a suspect and interrogate me with the help of your friends. And it's not like you've warmed up since then."

He was silent not knowing what to say. She was right. He held her at a distance because he didn't know what to do with her other than keep her safe.

She glanced around, avoiding eye contact with him. "Do you think I want a mate who doesn't want me? We're shifters, we have sex and walk away. I'm part vampire, too, so it's still a trait of that DNA. I just didn't think my *mate* would do that to me."

Aww, hell. Were those tears? She blinked rapidly, clearly not wanting him to notice. Not that he needed any more indication that she was different from Abigail. It had been clear from the start. His wife used her tears to control him, before and after she betrayed him.

"Shit." *Damn it*. Language. "I mean—"

Before he found a different word, she cut him off. "Don't worry, I can handle swearing, as long as they're adjectives and not aimed at me. I've just been upset with you and telling you to watch your language irritated you, so I kept doing it." She gave a sheepish lift of one shoulder.

If she could admit that, he could admit to his own poor behavior. "I'm sorry, okay? I want you every second of every day, and have ever since I laid eyes on you. But you've got to understand, this isn't easy for me."

"I know Bennett, I'm sorry—" Her tone was apologetic, too close to pity, so this time he cut her off.

"No, I've been an ass. You've been yourself and my head doesn't know if it can trust that. My heart doesn't dare. I thought I lost my chance at spending eternity with a mate after the first one found me lacking in every way, and would've rather seen me and my pack destroyed than just walk away. I wasn't supposed to have a chance with another mate again. It's never been heard of. I mean," he shoved a hand through his hair, "I accepted that I was going to go feral and die alone at the hands of my pack, trusting them to take me out before I hurt any innocents."

That was quite some emotional baggage he just threw at her. Now to just wait for her reaction.

"Okay…" she started slowly, "how about we start by trying to be friends?"

Friends? She didn't want *friendship* from this male. Yeah, okay, she did. But after she had his body…And his blood, don't forget his blood. Her beloved cows' blood was like drinking grape juice after having the rarest, most expensive wine in history.

"Would a friend drink my blood instead of a cow's?" He growled, heat filling his eyes, like he intended to pounce on her.

"Maybe," she drawled, her heartbeat picking up, "if it meant a lot to the friend."

Almost hoping, okay really hoping, they would have a romantic rendezvous right there in the middle of the woods, Spencer waited with breathless anticipation as Bennett stepped closer to her.

"When you need more blood, come to me." His deep voice vibrated over her nerve endings, making her shiver. "Don't tap the cows."

Oh, if only it were that easy. "Bennett," he scowled at the hint of argument in her tone, "I'm afraid if I keep taking your blood and shifting then I'll smell like a hybrid and it'll be harder to hide."

Bennett gave a curt nod, squinted up at the sun through the trees before turning to stalk toward her house.

"We better get planting," he said brusquely.

Disappointment fluttered through her and she frowned down at her shoes. Had she offended him? She'd take brooding Bennett barking orders and cussing every other word over ambivalent Bennett.

After asking her what needed to be done, he managed to avoid her for the next few hours. Lunch came and went; he made sandwiches, then wandered outside to eat his meat pile with a tiny piece of bread and left hers on the counter.

Sitting alone, wondering if she should get a blood meal from Tulip before heading back to the cabin, her phone rang.

"Hi Spencer! It's Constance." Not waiting for a greeting, Constance rushed on. "We finally have a contract drawn up. When's a good time for you to come look at it?"

Pausing to peer out her window and assess the weather, Spencer calculated when they could meet.

"Tomorrow afternoon would work well."

"Great! Stop by the store about two o'clock. You can take your time going over the contract and make any suggestions."

A thought popped into Spencer's head. "I might bring my…friend with. Is that okay?"

"The more the merrier. See you then." Constance's warm tone brightened Spencer's day.

"Who are you talking to?" Bennett was using his Guardian voice and there went Spencer's mood boost.

"The lady from the store I'll be selling my produce at needs to meet so I can read over and sign the contract. It's tomorrow at two." Spencer polished off her milk and stood to clear dishes, ignoring the dark form blocking the doorway.

Couldn't do it. He had his collar open revealing a sweaty chest, his jeans were dirty, and his hair was scattered like he just rolled out of bed. Which he had, hours ago. The blond scruff on his face highlighted the deep bronze his skin had taken on over the years, showcasing his square jaw and stern demeanor.

This was the real Bennett and she liked it.

"No way. They can email it or something." This was also the real Bennett and she didn't like it.

"I'm going in to meet with them, it's better for business. You're welcome to come along," she said, striving to keep her tone neutral. Reminding herself the Guardians were putting themselves in danger to protect her helped tamp down her fear they would lock her away for her own good.

"Hell yes, I'm coming. I'll talk to Commander Fitzsimmons and we'll come up with a game plan." Bennett was already leaving when she stopped him.

"Thank you."

He stilled, half turning back toward her. "For what?"

"For your pack protecting me. I don't take it lightly, and I won't do anything stupid to bring more trouble to your door."

His jaw clenched as he looked straight ahead. "That's what friends are for." Before she could ask him what he meant by that, he threw a work question at her. "I've got the north field going. Planted *flowers* with your vegetables. Now what?"

A small smile touched her face remembering his look of puzzlement when she handed him geraniums to plant amongst her tomatoes, that soon morphed into a dubious arched brow when she swore they would help keep pests away.

"I have two more bins of seedlings I need to get in today. Tomorrow morning, we can weed and spread the cow manure out on the area I'm prepping for late summer planting. It's pretty mineral deficient. Tomorrow afternoon will be dreary, and then it'll be rainy for almost two days. I can use those days to tend to my mushrooms. They're such divas. Next week will be sunny and pretty warm, with temps in the eighties and not much wind—"

Spencer was ticking off her to-do list in her head and staring out the window to gauge the weather, like she had been when talking to Constance. She didn't notice right away when Bennett pivoted to face her with his arms crossed and forehead creased.

"What?" she inquired.

"I haven't seen you watching the weather channel, so how do you know the ten-day forecast?" He regarded her like she asked him to plant beans in between the corn rows again.

"I know the land, and the weather seems to go along with it." Her innate gift was pretty worthless in her life on the run, but it was invaluable to her life in hiding.

"So you can talk to plants?" Now he wore the same expression as when he found her crushing egg shells, and she asked him to pour vinegar on them and sprinkle them around her tomato rows.

"Yeah, I ask them what they want for dinner and how much manure to sprinkle on them." She meant it in jest, but he scowled even harder. "I just have a sense of the weather patterns for the season, how healthy the land is, and what will grow best where. The other tips I've picked up from my parents and online organic gardening forums like Hippy Dippy Land Nut dot com."

"Your brother can freeze people *and* hear voices…you got anything else? Anything that's useful for keeping you alive?"

"Uh, no," she threw a little extra attitude in, "that's why I decided to hide instead and live in the boondocks. I barely have to go to town and can sell my product through intermediaries like Constance and her husband Mark."

"Sounds like a lonely life."

He didn't know the half of it. "Pretty much. At least planning my business has taken my mind off whether more of my family has been tortured or killed because of me."

"We can protect your parents, too." Bennett's pack had already discussed bringing her parents in. She was still considering it.

"I'm afraid to call them. Afraid they'll head to West Creek and Sigma will jump them expecting them to come since we have Ronnie, too."

He ran his hand through his hair and sighed. "All right. I'll go work on planting one bin of seedlings and talk with the boss about the plan for tomorrow."

Spencer watched him walk outside, his drool-worthy backside mesmerizing her. She never did get to see his naked behind as much as she'd like. She'd like to nip it, like he did to her when he was carrying her through the woods.

His mostly distant efforts relating with her, not to mention spending each night at the lodge, didn't give her any hope it would happen soon.

***

She was drinking from that fucking cow again, choosing Bessie today. His neck throbbed in tune with the bulge in his pants reminiscing about the ecstasy her bite brought him. She made her choice and he wasn't it.

Friends. He could be friendly.

That was a lie. He'd still been an ass to her since their talk the day before, but more of a protective ass than an outright one. The errand into town today fired up his nerves. They'd made three attempts to grab her since he'd met her, and now Sigma knew the Guardians had Ronnie. How many spies out on the town did they have?

At least Commander Fitzsimmons was on board with Bennett's protection detail. It took him away from regular duties, but the commander took family and pack protection seriously. The Guardians would be on standby in case the couple ran into trouble in town.

While Bennett dug in soil planting flowers and scattering egg shells, Master Bellamy had been warming up to Parrish. They couldn't have the kid go catatonic again, but they needed to find out what he knew, what his gifts were, and why he refused to be vocal. The more Bennett recalled Parrish's interchange before they questioned Spencer, the more he thought the kid was key to this whole mystery. Or at least a pathway to the key.

Climbing into the driver's seat of Spencer's truck, he readjusted himself in his jeans. Damn thing never tapered down around her, and it didn't help watching her trot in from the pasture wearing a simple blouse with capris and her hair clipped back. She was so young and fresh, he understood why she wanted to keep her distance from him. He would taint her with his bad history and years of plowing through women.

Didn't mean he had to like it. But he refused to change for anyone. He played good cop long enough, acting like the charmer and gentlemen he wasn't born to be. No more. He was done. Benjamin Young might have been willing to change himself for a woman, but not Bennett Young.

"I didn't have time to clean up," he called out the open window.

That wasn't true, he could've made time. He wouldn't have minded changing clothes since he was pretty gritty from planting that morning, plus he hadn't had time to shave before he had heard Spencer heading out for the day. Then he busted ass to get the rest of the plants in the ground—how many different kinds of lettuce were there?—while Spencer cleaned up. Here he was, sweaty and dirty, and about to go out in public. It had been decades since that happened.

Climbing into the passenger seat with no comment that he assumed the driver's position in her truck, she flashed him a rueful look. "You'll do."

"I know. Where's the store?"

Yep, he's a cocky bastard.

Spencer recited the directions, and they drove to town with the windows down to enjoy the fresh air, while rain clouds built on the horizon.

"Bennett, can you read over the contract after I'm done?"

Her request caught him off guard. He planned to drift around, ensuring her safety while committing the entire store's layout and surroundings to memory. Plus, he figured she wouldn't want his moody, grimy ass lingering near her while she solidified her contract.

"If you want me to," he finally said.

"Thanks. It's not like I can afford a lawyer, and I have no experience with these things. Buying the house and land was huge for me, and I swear if I was a full-blooded human, I'd have an ulcer eating a hole through me."

Did he just feel his male pride boost a notch or two? It wasn't like he hadn't been doing stuff for her for almost two weeks, working his tail off getting her produce planted, not to mention saving her. But that was because she had no choice about him hanging around. This request to help her was of her own free will, with no disclaimers about him cleaning up first or waiting in the truck until she called him.

The tiny organic store was situated in downtown West Creek. According to Spencer, they bought the attached building next to it and were in the process of expanding. That was a good sign for her.

She introduced him to the young owners. They appeared a little shell-shocked at having a tall, imposing male roam their store, but took it in stride. And he didn't miss the secretive grin Constance shot toward Spencer when she thought he wasn't looking.

Bennett read over the contract, made a few recommendations, listened to Spencer and Mark throw ideas around, before excusing himself to go check out the surroundings.

Wandering out the front door, Bennett rested against the brick wall by the entrance. A familiar sense of unease filtered through his consciousness. Retaining his nonchalance, he zeroed in individually on the people nearby, determining if they were innocents or threats.

A block away he caught sight of her. She was tall, her nearly black, short hair swept off shaved sides, with piercing green eyes. She wore a shirt his keen eyesight could read: "Little Red Riding Hood Was A Snitch." Agent X. Her expression was unreadable and that bothered him. Agent X always had an expression.

She made no move, just stood in plain sight facing the store. Bennett examined across the street from the Agent to find her partner, Agent E. Like Bennett, the tall, dark Agent was leaning up against a wall sipping from a coffee cup.

The two Agents met each other's gaze. Bennett tensed when Agent E crossed the street to meet up with his partner, but they both only meandered to a charcoal gray car and climbed in. Bennett scanned up and down the street but detected no other suspicious activity, and the two Agents stayed put.

Sigma was deadly, evil. X and E had always been a pain in the ass. They'd each killed shifters, which should piss off the Guardians, but none of them could argue that the shifters didn't earn what had happened to them. The shifters the Agents went after were ones the Guardians would have eventually dealt with.

Last year, Agent E took out one of their fellow Guardians, Mason, but in doing so had saved Dani. It was so they could try to capture her, but if they hadn't intervened, Bennett would no doubt have a partner to nurse through losing a mate, much like Mercury had done for him.

What were the Agents up to, and why allow themselves to be seen? He was out by himself with their target, they could have jumped him. It'd take more than those two, but they had time to call reinforcements. These two Sigma Agents created trouble for shifters, especially interfering with

Guardians. They were good at their work, but they'd never been senselessly violent. Regardless, Bennett expected trouble.

Boss, we're wrapping it up here. X and E are on the radar. I'll have to lose their tail heading back.

Man, it was so much nicer to mind-speak, like the good ol' days. They still used their phones, cuz hello, having the internet at your fingertips was awesome. No more bulky radios made missions run smoother.

Roger. I'll head out with Jace and Kaitlyn to watch Spencer's place.

Bennett bet he would. The commander didn't take X's interference lightly, and they were all under strict orders to let him deal with her. Sometimes Bennett wondered about the commander's obsession with the naughty Agent. In fact, he suspected—

"Ready?" Spencer strode out, stopping after spotting Bennett.

"Let's go." Heading to her pickup Bennett took one last glance down the street to the car the two Agents were planted in.

"What's wrong?" Spencer sensed his serious mood.

"Get in and I'll talk to you on the way back."

Bennett had to give her credit. She didn't immediately rubber-neck all around her. He could see her discreetly inspecting the surrounding businesses and shoppers like he had done. After they were both in the pickup, she used the mirrors to look around.

"Where are they?" she asked.

"A block back, dark gray car. Two Agents."

"Can you lose them?"

"Let's see."

He sensed fear spike within Spencer.

Twisting and turning through town, the car kept pace. It was the middle of the day. Bennett couldn't race through the streets and cut off other drivers without endangering innocent people or attracting human law enforcement.

Spencer sat stiffly beside him, fear and sadness radiating off her. "Now I might have put Mark and Constance in danger. I'll never be free of them. Not until I'm dead."

Chapter Eleven

Spencer trudged into her house, taking the clip out of her hair. It took them almost an hour to lose their Sigma tail. An hour of riding on pins and needles. What if they couldn't lose the Agents? An hour of worry for her new friends. Maybe she should call them tomorrow, to make sure they weren't tortured for information. A pit formed in her gut just thinking about more people getting hurt because of her.

Bennett had been quiet the entire drive, concentrating on driving without incident while evading the Agents. His determination and stubbornness were palpable, but otherwise she had no idea what was going on with him.

It was sprinkling outside, soon it would be a steady rain. Ordinarily, she would love a rainy day to diddle around the house, start more seedlings, tend to her mushrooms, or just read. But now she had to think about running again, giving up her dream of having a home. It seemed like too much of a fantasy to be able to talk to her brother, face-to-face even, more in the last week than the last seven years since she'd left home.

Bennett came in the door behind her after parking her pickup in the shop. She didn't turn to face him, instead she stared out the kitchen window above the sink, afraid she might burst into tears thinking about what other fantasies she would have to give up leaving him.

He was surly, brooding, and bossy, but he was real. He was genuine with her and she sensed his angst that it would drive her away. He couldn't see in himself what she did, like his loyalty and honor, and his compassion for his job and loved ones. Just because he sensed she was his mate, despite his history, he stayed by her side, caring for her and her land, to make sure she was safe. He was as stunning inside as he was outside.

He came up behind her, resting his hands on her upper arms and leaning his head down, burrowing into her hair. Spencer closed her eyes and sank back into him, enjoying the quiet intimacy of the moment.

Reaching up, Bennett ran his fingers through her hair, letting it fall back gently onto her shoulders. Kissing her neck through the curtain of hair, he skimmed his hands around her waist and unhooked her capri buttons.

Anticipation of Bennett's hands on her bare skin caused Spencer lightly wiggle her hips to help get her pants down faster.

A soft chuckle came from behind. "My little hybrid needs some attention."

Spencer was about to respond when his fingers found her folds. Massaging her with one hand, she sensed him undoing his jeans with the other.

"Keep your hands on the counter.," His breath tickled her ear, she shivered against his chest, his digits worked her faster. "Let me do everything."

Once his pants were undone, he eased her hips back, bending her over the sink. Standing on her tip-toes wet and ready for him, she groaned, waiting as he placed himself to enter. With a smooth thrust, he slid into her as deeply as possible.

They both stilled, enjoying the feeling of being together, his head still buried in her neck. Deep inside he twitched and his fingers started moving again.

It didn't take much to push Spencer over the edge, holding onto the sink, crying out Bennett's name.

When she was done, coming down from the tumultuous high, Bennett secured her hips and pounded against her. Hands still gripping the sink, she moved with his thrusts preparing to join him in his climax.

When he arched his back and dug his fingers into her hips, he roared her name, shuddering inside of her. The maelstrom of his release, the feeling of him filling her, sent her into another climax with him.

Panting over the edge of the sink, her legs shaky, with Bennett leaning over her, still inside and holding her hips, she attempted to calm her breath.

She thought Bennett was doing the same until he withdrew from her and leaned down to take her pants off the rest of the way.

Yes.

He wasn't done yet. That was the worst part about being out on her own and not fully human. It was difficult to find temporary partners who satisfied her. This male would be all she needed.

Kicking off his own pants and stripping off his shirt, he spun her around and lifted her shirt up and off, too.

"I haven't tasted you yet," he growled, the fierce, hot look in his eyes saying he wasn't near to being done.

Her pulse picked up when the meaning of his words sunk in. Before she could strategize where, he lifted her up onto the counter next to the sink. He gave her a long lingering kiss before sinking to his knees and lifting her legs over his shoulders.

In an incredibly sweet gesture, he kissed his way up her thigh to her center, where she wanted him the most. Tunneling her hands through his hair, earning a little rumble of pleasure from him, she held on while his licked and kissed and nipped her to a peak of ecstasy she'd never reached before. Drawing her knees higher, she was afraid she would rip out his hair when she came more powerfully than ever before, crying his name.

He rose, sporting what could only be described as a wolfish grin, and drove himself deep into her.

"My mate liked that?" he asked with false innocence.

"Your mate liked it a lot." She gasped, still catching her breath while he stroked her to another peak.

The grin faded to an intense heat as he dropped his lips to hers. They explored each other's mouth, dueling tongues vying for every scrap of pleasure the other could give.

She held him tightly, their mouths locked together as they moaned their release into each other.

Letting the shudders subside, he kissed her tenderly as if this was the last time they could be together. And he was right. She would have to go to keep those she loved safe. And she loved her mate. No doubt about it.

Tears pricked the back of her eyelids. He released her mouth, but their bodies remained locked together.

Opening her eyes to soak in the depth of his navy blue stare, the tears fell free when he reached up to tenderly wipe dry the corners of her eyes.

"I haven't made love to anyone for over a hundred years." The insecurity in his look almost advanced her to fully sobbing. "I haven't let anyone touch me or kiss me, let alone lay in a bed to make love in the traditional sense."

"It's okay, Bennett. I understand." She did, but her heart broke just a little at his confession, wishing that she had time to wait for the day he trusted what was between them. "We can take it slow."

It was an odd offering considering they were still locked in an embrace with him still half hard inside of her.

"I don't want to take it slow." His voice became harsh, determined. "I don't want to be friends. I want to be your mate. I want to run with you in the woods, and I want you to drink from me and not from those damn cows."

The tears kept rolling at his confession. Her heart shattered. "I want it all, too," she cried. "But I can't stay here and you can't leave."

Tenderly wiping the tears from her cheeks, he shushed her until the hiccup-sobs subsided.

"This is what we're going to do." He withdrew himself from her and swept her up into his arms to head toward her bedroom. "I'm going to make slow, sweet love to you, while I'm on top, even."

Spencer allowed herself a small self-satisfied grin, snuggling into him more.

"Then we'll talk, because I have an idea."

***

Bennett strolled into Pale Moonlight shaking the rain off himself. Dipping his chin toward the imposing owner of the club, Christian, he settled himself at the bar. He could see his clean cut, clean shaven reflection in the mirror across the bar.

His usual Belgian ale slid in front of him and he tipped his head to the female bartender, a member of Christian's pack who had worked there for years.

Drinking deeply from his mug, he swiveled on his stool to eye the dance floor. Another member of Christian's pack, a male named Weston, roamed the dance floor catching women's attention.

Weston glanced up at Bennett and lifted a questioning brow. Bennett passed him a knowing nod and finished off his beer as he watched Weston work the crowd.

The muscular male was turning enough female heads, but he zeroed on one, a woman with long, dark hair and barely any clothes, except see-through leggings and a sheer top. She pressed into the male as he whispered in her ear. She searched the bar area until her eyes landed on Bennett.

He calmly gazed back at her, awaiting her decision. He saw the hitch in her breath, the moment of indecision, and Weston murmur seductively in her ear while stroking her hips. The woman bit her lip and leaned back into him giving her acquiescence.

Putting his mug down, Bennett kept his eyes on the couple, following them to The Den. Weston entered a backroom Bennett was very familiar with.

"Hey," the woman said breezily, eyeballing Bennett's designer label clad body while she was glued to Weston's. "What's your name?"

"Bennett Young." He gave his full name. And for good measure, "Say it."

Her pupils dilated and her cheeks flushed with desire. "Nice to meet you, Bennett Young."

She glided toward Bennett, but Weston pulled her back into his embrace, kissing her deeply while Bennett closed them into the room.

A tall form moved out from the darkened corner of the room, and Bennett stepped back to make room for the sinister-looking male.

Weston let the girl go, spinning her to face where Bennett once stood, but now Jace waited calmly.

She gasped, fear permeating the air, but Jace quickly calmed her, locking his ice blue gaze on her. "I'm not going to hurt you. I'm not even here." His mesmerizing voice captured the woman's attention, hypnotizing her. Bennett had to admire how much the Guardian had grown in his power. "When you leave here, you will think, you will *remember*, having sex with Bennett."

She nodded mindlessly.

"You want to have sex with these guys?"
She nodded again.

"Go to it," Jace finished, stepping aside.

Bennett moved to hang out behind the woman when Weston pulled her leggings down her thighs. As he sat down, she kneeled and unclasped the male's pants.

It was critical that Bennett remain behind the woman, at least during this part, Jace had said when they were making plans for tonight. But it didn't mean it was comfortable. It was not like he wasn't used to being around others having sex, but he usually had a role. This felt...weird, just standing here, waiting for her to finish blowing Weston.

Jace settled in next to him, speaking low enough so the woman with her human ears couldn't hear, "Everybody in place at the house?"

"Yeah, the boss said we do this for a few nights. If Sigma doesn't hit us now, they're planning a different move." And that would be bad. An attack on Spencer and her house was something they could plan for, but he couldn't hang out at the club each and every night. Bennett couldn't come here each night putting on a show or eventually they'd get busted. "Cassie pissed about you doing this?"

"Nah, she gets it." Jace blew out a breath, trying not to look at the couple while the smell of desire filled the air. "Besides, she has some continuing education to do and claims I keep *distracting* her."

Bennett snorted. "What? She can't study on her back?"

Jace chuckled wickedly. The male's human mate had transitioned into their world pretty well, but it didn't matter what the species, living with an alpha male shifter could be physically demanding.

"No man, her sitting there, with that studious look on her face, intent on the laptop…gets me going every time." Jace directed his attention to the woman, using his mesmerizing voice to describe what she would remember Bennett doing to her, while Bennett himself never laid a hand, or any other body part, on her.

"You said you're going back to school to get your master's in finance. Does watching you study have the same effect on her?" Bennett's tone was laced with humor, but he fought an all-out grin at Jace's reaction to his question.

"She likes 'em smart. Why do you think I'm still taking classes?" Jace didn't bother fighting his own grin, his fangs lengthening slightly.

"Dude, I'm so good, I don't even have to touch her," Bennett joked about the woman moaning.

"Right, only cuz I'm telling her how good you should be."

Weston's withdrawn groan signaled his finish and the high-pitched whine signaled the woman's. Staring at the ceiling, out of the corner of his eye Bennett could see Weston pull the woman onto his lap, pull her leggings all the way off, and settle her on his length.

Most of Bennett's role was done, but he couldn't leave. Simultaneously, he and Jace turned around to stare at the other wall to give the couple a modicum of privacy.

"How many girls we gotta go through tonight?" Jace asked.

Bennett exhaled, thinking about his long, long talk with the commander. "At least two, but if we can do three, it would be best. Weston's up for it."

The commander's phone call to Christian solved the dilemma of who would help thoroughly scent the girls with sex. Commander Fitzsimmons grimly said he would step in, but hated taking another Guardian from Spencer's protection detail. Bennett suspected his commander just wasn't interested in random sex and would've dragged his feet to the club out of a sense of duty.

Thankfully, the phone call to Christian planning this charade ended with him offering up a member of his pack who would be willing to play and could be trusted. Jace, having been a member of Christian's pack before he met Cassie and was recruited by the Guardians, vouched for Weston.

When Bennett frequented The Den, he was known for going all night. Now he just wanted to go home. But in order for Sigma's spies to question any assumption the hybrid they were searching for might be Bennett's mate, he needed to act like a single Guardian.

"I would tell her to walk out like her legs were numb, but from the sounds of it, I think Weston is taking care of that," Jace said wryly.

The piercing, deep shriek of climax, followed by Weston's grunts, signaled the end to this woman. Bennett would have to be seen walking her out and recruiting the next candidate.

Gritting his teeth and gutting through it, he accepted the woman's arm after she got her leggings back on and helped her back out to the dance floor. He quickly caught the next female's eye but skipped over her. She was a shifter and their ruse wouldn't work as well with her. Next up, a short, dark haired female he didn't think he'd had before was looking his way.

Picking her up next, she followed him into the room. Putting the night on repeat, Jace wove his magic, Weston worked the girl, and hopefully any Sigma plants in the club would report back that Bennett was still hitting up the back rooms of the club so when Spencer died, they left her dead.

Chapter Twelve

There's movement, get back here.
Commander Fitzsimmons sent his
mental thought to Bennett as soon as he felt the
faint vibrations in the air. Rhys was sitting on front
deck of Spencer's house staring out into the night
while she was stationed inside with her trusty
shotgun. The light rain had quit before making the
ground soggy, and that would be good in case there
was fighting.

Bennett convinced Apollo to stay at the
cabin babysitting the kittens. They couldn't plan the
dog's nature to rescue Spencer into this set-up.
Apollo was too unpredictable in a scheme of events
that were already a giant unknown as it was.

Kaitlyn was positioned at the edge of
Spencer's land, Mercury was camped on the back
porch, Ronnie was waiting in the tree line, and Doc
Garreth was on standby at the infirmary. Spencer's
brother had taken quite an interest in Doc's
business, and as for the healer, he seemed to enjoy
researching the latest must-haves in research
equipment and brainstorming ideas to obtain
materials with Ronnie.

Dani said there's at least seven bodies roaming the woods, three fast moving, possible vamps or maybe only enhanced Agents. Mercury's voice drifted through the commander's mind. After Dante's birth, Dani lost the ability to talk with the rest of the Guardians, but at least her connection to Mercury remained. Maybe over time it would grow stronger again. Until then, she normally texted, but silence was golden for this mission so she sent her messages through Mercury.

Seven. Damn. They expected as much. Two failed missions striving to take Spencer in her house would cause Sigma to attack heavy. They didn't waste their vampire Agents. The human Agents were getting to be a dime a dozen. Madame G was growing more frantic in her search for Spencer so she had no problem throwing away their lives due to lack of training.

Dani spotted Agents X and E, boss.

Fuck.

Just fuck.

Location? Commander Fitzsimmons couldn't lose any more Guardians to the Agents and while he couldn't see either X or E killing Spencer outright, they could cause enough of a problem that could end up getting her killed. Or maybe they'd capture her and let someone else do the dirty work.

A thought occurred to Commander Fitzsimmons. It had been awhile since he'd crossed paths with X and some things had changed. It was worth a shot.

Nice of you to join us.

A throaty, surprised laugh drifted through his mind making his shaft tighten and that was a shitty problem to have with the Agent.

My, my Rhys, you have a shiny, new talent. She always called him by his first name. He hated the intimate feel to it. And he hated that it was probably the reason why she did it.

What are you up to? Mind-speak wasn't a new trick, just one that didn't work until recently.

I'm about six feet tall. Another husky chuckle at her own joke rolled through his brain straight down to his cock. He really didn't need this tonight.

How's Demetrius? Commander Fitzsimmons could get his digs in, too.

Silence followed for several seconds. *Do you think you can keep this girl from getting killed?* There was no hint of a taunt, she posed a serious question.

Yes.

You do that then. It was like a mental door slammed between him and his connection to her.

Commander Fitzsimmons rubbed his face and sighed. He should give up trying to figure out what X and her partner were up to, but he couldn't shake the feeling that it was critical, to all of them.

***

Spencer was shaking in her cowboy boots. The Guardians kept her in on their mental transmissions and she heard how many Agents were out there. Was this going to work? Where was Bennett?

The lights in her house were off, darkness settled deep into the corners this far out of town. There had been no need for Sigma to cut the power, but it was meant to unnerve her and distract the Guardians. The problem with human Agents was that they strategized like humans. She could see as well as a full-blood in the dark. The Guardians took it all into account and it became part of the plan.

She walked out the back door carrying her shotgun, passing Mercury who was sitting on the back porch. "I'm going to fill the generator and start it up."

"You should get back inside. I can do it." He moved in a half-hearted effort to get up.

"No, I got it, just keep protecting me," she reassured him, sticking to the script.

Leaning her shotgun against the outside of her house, she went over to the red gas cans and picked one up. Making a great show of filling the generator by the back corner of the house, utilizing her unique cussing method while creating a spectacle of spilling gas while trying to get the generator filled.

"Aw, heck, Mercury. I spilled gas all over myself. I need to go get changed before I start this thing up." She attempted to make her announcement loud enough without being terribly obvious.

Mercury just grunted, facing out into the night.

Just as she was about to enter the backdoor, Mercury popped up with his gun raised, firing into the trees. "Get down, Spencer!"

She dove into the house, landing on her belly and rolling into the wall, knocking the breath from her. Dazed, she struggled to her hands and knees trying to get her bearings.

Sounds of gunfire surrounded her house. Commander Fitzsimmons ambushed from the front like Mercury was from the back.

Trying not to panic, Spencer strained to keep her breathing even, reminding herself that this was part of the plan, and these males and lone female were trained for this.

Spencer released a shriek that was more nerves than fear when a round of bullets shattered the kitchen window, destroying the decorations she'd hung on her wall. Not having much time to resign herself to losing everything, she certainly didn't want to witness the destruction of her items. Not that she had much that was sentimental having lived a transient life, but this run-down house had been hers, and the items inside, while purchased used and well-worn, were also hers.

Keeping low, Spencer scooted against an interior wall. She didn't know yet if she'd leave through the front door or the back, so she centered herself as best she could in the house waiting for the commander's signal.

Oh, fudge! She'd forgotten her shotgun out back by the generator. It was more for show, but what if their plan took a detour and she found herself facing an Agent?

Spencer! The fear in Bennett's voice shot through her head.

I'm okay. I think there's a lot of them out there.

We're almost there. Keep your head down.

The mental communication was shut down, and Spencer couldn't wait for Bennett and Jace to arrive. She was onboard with making a scene of dying in front of all these Agents, but not if it meant one or more of the Guardians getting killed. With these odds, it wasn't looking like one could happen without the other.

I've lost track of the vampire. A woman's voice mentally warned everyone, including Spencer. Son of a gun, a vampire! That one would be harder to kill and its heightened senses might be harder to fool about her faux death.

The commander's voice filtered in, strong, but grim. *That makes eight Agents total, one's a vampire, X is a shifter, and X's partner E. The other five might not be so highly trained. I took down one in the tree line but I don't know if he'll stay down.*

I've hit two, but one's started twitching. We need to roast 'em soon before I have to put them down again. This time it was Mercury.

Injuries?

Nothing serious, boss. You?

Superficial, the commander responded. *Kaitlyn, you got eyes on the side of the house Mercury and I can't cover?*

That's where the vamp was stalking. I can't see him anymore. I'm moving closer. The female Guardian was concealed deep in the trees, and apparently the vampire was closer to the house than the rest thought.

Signs of X and E?

Dani only spotted them once, she hasn't seen them cross her surveillance since, came Mercury's reply.

The Guardians had briefed her on Agents X and E after the car chase. Spencer's parents had taught her about Madame G's complete domination of her people. The other Sigma chapters didn't always use a letter system for their Agents, and they weren't nearly as sadistic to their own people as the madwoman in charge of this chapter. Yet oddly enough, she never ran out of recruits offering themselves up to her.

Spencer almost jumped out of her skin when the back door opened and Mercury slid in her gun. The handle sailed toward her so she only had to scoot back a short distance to grab it, instantly feeling better once the familiar wood hilt was in her hands.

Spencer, signal us immediately if you sense anything at all.

Yes, sir.

Except for a few spurts of gunfire, everything was quiet. Spencer almost preferred the mayhem of the shoot-out. This was too quiet.

Trying to think strategically, she had figure out how and where a vampire would get into her house. Her kitchen window was obvious, but Ronnie was hidden in the tree line on that side of the house and would've alerted them if he saw anything. Otherwise, the commander and Mercury could both cover that end of the house from where they were stationed.

The bedroom windows were on the back of the house where Mercury was, so that left the end with the attached garage. The far wall of the garage had no window, that's why with only three Guardians, they left it undefended. She rigged a bell to the door into her house from the garage. So far, that had remained silent.

Where would a fast-moving paranormal creature gain entrance unseen into her house? One of the windows, maybe when the Guardians were distracted in a different direction? It would be hard, even in the dark to sneak into a high window—

Oh, crap! The basement windows. Her dank, rundown basement, that was barely a step above a root cellar, had small rectangular windows. The shoot-out was to distract Commander Fitzsimmons and Mercury, so the vampire could flash next to the foundation and slide through the window.

Spencer jumped up and spun to bring her shotgun up to aim at the basement door. She had almost forgotten it was there because the rest of the house had demanded so much of her attention.

A tall, thin figure loomed in front of her and pushed the shotgun barrel out of the way just as she pulled the trigger. The recoil from the new angle of her gun pushed her back, and she bumped up hard against the wall. Chaos erupted from outside. She heard Mercury and the commander simultaneously dive for cover as a barrage of bullets pelleted the house, keeping them from coming to her rescue.

The male vampire hissed at her, displaying his fangs, probably to scare her. But while she smelled human, he'd forgotten she had a set of her own.

Letting them drop, she hissed back at him and he snickered at her.

"You will be fun. I can't wait to taste you, hybrid." His greedy, red-glowing eyes bored into her.

An explosion rocked the house. Both her and the vampire swung their heads toward the back corner.

Flames flickered through the windows down the hall. They hit the generator and gas stockpile with some kind of explosive. Her house would be toast in a few minutes, and she couldn't get out yet.

Flipping her gun around and catching the barrel, she used her superhuman speed to swing it like a baseball bat at the vampire's head.

The hilt of the weapon caught the side of his head. Since it had been years since she'd unleashed her strength, the power of the blow caught both of them by surprise.

The vampire flew into the wall but righted himself immediately, shaking his head.

Between Spencer's strength and the vampire's hard head, the handle of her gun split. Seizing the offering of an impromptu stake, she wrenched it apart to pry a piece free.

The male lunged for her, fangs bared, aiming for her neck when a loud bang stopped them both short.

Hunched over her gun, she spared a look around. The gunfire came from inside the house. Had one of the Guardians come to her rescue?

A red dot bloomed in between the vampire's eyes, and he toppled over at her feet.

Mouth open in shock, Spencer glanced up and her heart sank. Standing at the entrance of her basement was not Commander Fitzsimmons, nor Mercury. Nor was the tall, wide male any other Guardian. That meant he was one of the bad guys.

This male didn't smell quite human, but he wasn't a shifter or vampire, that much she could tell over the smoke building inside the house. The fire licked at the walls. Double dang, she had no weapon and nowhere to run. If she ran outside and got shot, she should heal, and although she was willing to test it, it would threaten their plan.

Before she could decide, the male spoke, pinning her with his black eyes. "Have you called for them yet?"

Confusion built at his words. "What?"

"The Guardians. Have you told them we've gotten in the house yet?" he repeated, impatiently. "If you haven't, do it now." Then he leaned down and opened up a Zippo to light the vampire's clothing on fire, intending to destroy the creature for good. The smoke coming off the vampire getting dusted mingled with the encroaching smoke of the generator fire as it burned its way into Spencer's house.

Gaping at the Agent, Spencer worked on arranging her scrambled thoughts and realized he was right. *They're in the house!*

"Did you do it?" he asked again.

"Yes." She remained still, planning her next move, struggling to breathe through the thickening smoke.

"Good. For what it's worth, I'm sorry." The man shoved past her, heading for the front door, kicked it open, and raised his odd-looking gun, aiming it at Spencer.

Spencer tensed to dive down the hallway. The bang resounded and a burn ripped through her shoulder. As she dropped to the floor, the smoldering of the highly combustible vampire fully ignited and flared. She used her good hand to cover her mouth and nose with her shirt before lack of oxygen from the thick smoke knocked her out. She pushed herself toward the back door on her butt when she heard the hiss of the body before it exploded.

Bennett leaned out the window and used his firearm to gun down an Agent standing in the driveway shooting at Commander Fitzsimmons. Intent on his target, not hearing the SUV bearing down on him, the Agent went down and Jace ran him over for good measure. They'd have to burn him later.

Jace skidded to a halt and both males hopped out, guns blazing, giving Mercury and the commander some relief.

"We've got to get Spencer out!" Bennett shouted.

Jace shot him a warning look. Yeah, yeah, stick to the plan. But the back of the house was in flames, and it wouldn't be long before the rest of the old dwelling took on the fire and smoke filled the rooms too much for Spencer to safely escape when it was time.

Everything in Bennett froze in fear and rage when Agent E kicked open the front door and turned to shoot Spencer. Bennett watched as his mate dropped.

"Nooo!" Bennett sprinted for cabin.

He saw Ronnie ease around the tree he was hiding behind, whipping his hands around. *You need to stop, Bennett. Don't go in there!*

She needs help getting out.

~178~

We need to try this. Stop!

Bennett kept running, regardless of Agent E turning on him with his weapon. The Agent was ready to fire, but he froze. As in quit moving. And so did Bennett. Their immobility was thanks to Ronnie. Bennett strained against his own body, but couldn't move. In his periphery, he saw the commander stilled in mid-leap toward Agent E. Jace froze behind him.

Either Ronnie fucked up and spread his power's net too far or he made the command decision to freeze everybody.

Ronnie! Let me get her! Bennett roared at the male but was ignored. The male was huffing, shaking from holding that many bodies immobile.

Bennett remained immobile, mid-stride, helpless as the roof caught fire and more smoke filled the house. He didn't see Spencer rise, much less leave. Dread filled him as it dawned on him that not only did Agent E shoot her, but it may have been fatal.

Spencer! Spencer! Bennett screamed hard, almost blacking himself out with the power.

His mate was injured and unable escape a burning building, and he realized that the guilt all those years ago had been unfounded. He assumed the blame when everything that happened was on Abigail.

If she had been a decent human being, how could his wife have stood there and watched him be tortured and humiliated, even using his love for her to coerce him into obeying his captors? While she intended to be a good person, her fear and distrust allowed her to become corrupted. Bennett had gathered the best of himself and laid it all her feet, and it wasn't enough for her. She wasn't only willing to hurt him, but the males he called family. He would have never been what she desired.

Fuck, he'd barely had anything to do with Master Bellamy since his rescue. The male had risked his relationship with Bennett to save him because he knew what Bennett hadn't—that having to kill his own mate, along with the guilt of her betrayal, would've driven him feral.

A trickle of awareness pricked his brain. He caught pain and fear emanating from his mate, and readied to direct any power he did have to knocking Ronnie out so he could get to Spencer.

Calm down, Bennett. You totally owe me. Kaitlyn's determined voice raised that deadly emotion in Bennett's chest—hope.

She must've been out of range when Ronnie cast out his power and darted into the back door of the house to save Spencer while the others couldn't move and the Agents were immobilized where they couldn't view either entrance.

Bennett watched the tall female lift Spencer's limp body up onto her shoulders and trot out, both of them getting licked by the flames.

The building burned, and they were all helpless, mere observers.

Clear, came Kaitlyn's breathless voice. He could almost hear her mentally coughing as she struggled to hold in her physical coughing to remain undetected.

Ronnie went down in a heap as Bennett stumbled, but remained upright. He was free of Ronnie's hold. So were the rest of them. The creaking of the timbers was the only warning they had before the house tumbled in onto itself.

Agent E darted off the porch, out of Bennett's reach, heading for the woods. Commander Fitzsimmons' tackled Bennett to keep him from running after Spencer. Since that fell in line with their plan, and his mate was no longer in the burning wreckage, Bennett allowed himself to be taken to the ground with the commander pinning him down.

The wind picked up, but Bennett knew it wasn't a natural wind. Jace's voice spoke low on Mercury's conjured breeze. The words were meant to influence the remaining Agents into thinking Spencer had died in the fire. They didn't know if it would work, or if it was necessary, but both males' power had grown significantly since they mated so they could utilize it, especially for something as critical as this.

As it was, Bennett had to convince himself he saw Kaitlyn rescue Spencer, or his mind would fall for Jace's words.

"We need to gather the fallen Agents' bodies and drop them in the fire. Go check on

Ronnie." The commander jumped off Bennett and jogged to the closest body, which happened to be the one Jace ran over in the driveway.

Bennett hauled himself up, gave the house one last look. She was safe. Probably unconscious, but safe. And she would heal, she had to.

He wanted to rush to the lodge, dogging Kaitlyn's footsteps, and get his hands on his mate for himself, be with her every step of the way, hear what Doc Garreth had to say about her injuries, and never leave her side.

But if he did that, and any surviving Sigma Agent's saw, their ruse would be discovered. He had to play the role of Guardian, not concerned mate.

The wind died down and Bennett reached Ronnie. The young male was holding his head groaning.

Standing over the writhing form, Bennett visually checked him over. "You okay?"

"Ahh! No, Bennett. My head fucking hurts. Holding you down gave me the most massive hangover ever. Without the fun of the party!"

Ronnie was fine.

"Come on, kid. Let's get you to the lodge." It would give Bennett an excuse to get back there and find Spencer.

The others accounted for most all of the Agents, except the vampire, X and E, and one other. They would be the hardest beings to get to fall for Spencer's faked death. As far as Bennett could tell, and Mercury vouched for his side of the house, any Agents standing were either down or not looking at the house when Kaitlyn carried Spencer out.

The commander said the vampire could've been in the house, but he firmly denied Agent X had been close by. Bennett chose not to wonder how the commander could be so sure.

"Stick close, Ronnie. We'll head back, but there's still some Sigma garbage roaming these woods."

"You're kinda bossy," Ronnie huffed. This guy was basically his brother-in-law. If he didn't know how to clean-up some *Halo* alien scum, Bennett might've just left him behind.

"I'm protecting your ass."

"It's not my ass you're worried about."

"Nope, so let's go."

"You go. I want to help haul the dead to the fire."

Bennett nodded and checked in with the commander before leaving the kid behind. Okay, he wasn't a kid, but to Bennett he seemed so young, a little off-kilter, and he was Spencer's little brother. Ronnie was taking more and more interest in Guardian duties. While Bennett didn't think he'd ever be field material, they sure could use more support at the lodge. Doc Garreth was diligently working on building a research lab and Dani was improving and updating security, but they were quickly becoming a bigger pack with a lot of area to cover. They seemed to have a significantly large

Sigma threat to deal with and Ronnie could be a welcome addition.

Even if they took Madame G down, the organization was like Medusa's hair, another snake to take her place. With the West Creek Guardians growing in size and power, it'd just be a magnet for Sigma, like a gauntlet thrown down. Aside from Sigma, the heavily wooded hilly terrain provided a lot of cover for shifter packs, and Freemont and West Creek attracted a lot of shifters looking to live a modern life.

No, they wouldn't be going anywhere soon, especially if they could keep Spencer dead until they found out why Madame G wanted her that way.

How is she?

Chapter Thirteen

*G*roggy.

Spencer heard the female's mental reply as she bounced on the strong back of the Guardian. Her shoulder was on fire and hanging upside down didn't help. Her lungs probably resembled burnt toast, but each breath she took was a little less labored than the previous one.

Bennett said he'd meet them at the lodge; she wanted him now. Of course, she understood why they needed to keep their distance. Understood it, but hated it. Just like she hated sending him off to the club to act like his former self. Sure, she knew he wasn't going to do anything, but she was still one-half paranormal and that half didn't like their mate getting hit on. That half claimed mates for the world to see and nearly killed any being that interfered. So, no, she didn't like having to hide their relationship from the world. Her biting him to drink didn't mark him like a shifter's mark, and so he remained unscented with her claim. And that irritated her.

There were surviving Agents, Kaitlyn. I'll shift and come cover you.

He didn't speak into her mind directly, but opened his communication up so Spencer could hear if she was conscious. And she was, barely. When strong hands grabbed her and picked her up, there had been no fight left, the smoke having stolen all the air from her. The burn of the bullet robbed her strength, and Spencer suspected the worst. It was silver.

"Thanks for saving me, no-fraternizing-Kaitlyn."

Kaitlyn chuckled and stopped to set Spencer on her feet. "My reputation precedes me, as usual. Can you walk? I can protect us better with two hands and your ass out of the way."

The tall redhead had her hair in a long braid down her back, was utterly gorgeous, and carried what looked like a sniper rifle on her other shoulder. She had a handgun at the ready in case they ran into trouble.

"I can walk and I appreciate you not biting my ass like Bennett does when he carries me like that."

"If I thought you wouldn't mind, I would've totally nipped you."

Spencer wanly smiled at the Guardian's humor. Kaitlyn looked her over with a keen eye. "That bullet hole probably hurts like hell, but you look worse than you should. Any other injuries?"

"Silver," Spencer sighed, glancing around as Kaitlyn swore under her breath. "But I don't think the bullet is still in me. I think it went all the way through."

"Let's hope the vampire part of you laughs at the metal. Let's keep moving, stay in front of me; they're most likely behind us or beside us."

That didn't make Spencer feel better but she obeyed the Guardian. "I think the human part of me isn't tolerating the bullet wound as well, though." Spencer tried not to sway on her feet, didn't want to be even more of a burden than she was.

"The vampire part of you needs blood. Bennett's on his way. I'd offer, but he'd get a little bitchy. Why is the human part so dominant? It usually gets shoved aside by the shifter genes."

"Maybe there's too many species in my system," Spencer said wryly.

A twig snapped. "Get down!" Spencer had dropped to the ground even before Kaitlyn got her order out.

A thunk in the tree trunk over Spencer's head drew her attention, showing a crossbolt vibrating imperceptibly from the impact. Thank the Sweet Mother she had inhuman reflexes. Who the heck used crossbows nowadays? They were quiet, but so were silencers.

Oh, yeah. A group hunting a part-vampire. Spencer was pretty sure a stake through her heart would be harder to rebound from than the silver bullet.

Kaitlyn opened fire in the direction of the shooter when gunshots from another direction sent bark flying off a tree behind her. Sigma planted backup Agents in the trees, just in case the first team failed.

Spencer had no weapons and didn't know if she could shift with her shoulder out of commission. Then Kaitlyn squatted down in front of Spencer, sandwiching her between the tree and her much taller body. Pulling another gun out from her boot, she handed it to Spencer.

"Thanks." She breathed easier with a little defense.

"Make sure I get it back." Kaitlyn threw over her shoulder, regarding the trees around them. "I won it in a bet off a shifter at the club, and I'm going to take a selfie with it to send him."

Spencer fought a grin. This wasn't the appropriate time, dang it, but obviously this female was a riot. At least Bennett had one interlude with the opposite sex that didn't leave him shattered, or not bothering to even remember. Spencer didn't quite recall details of her handful of one night stands, but at least they'd had some conversation. She had even gotten their names and none of them tried to kill her. Imagine meeting only one of those criteria each time?

The crack of a branch to the left had both females raising their guns in the same direction.

"Cover the other side," Kaitlyn hissed, squeezing off three quick rounds.

Oh dang. Spencer realized her strategic failure when she whipped her head around and stared down a barrel held in front of a maliciously grinning face.

Before Spencer could open her mouth to tell Kaitlyn to move, a light colored wolf jumped at the arm holding the gun. The crack of bone and cry of pain sounded at the same time as the gunshot, but Bennett's attack sent the bullet out into the trees instead of her direction.

Growling from the wolf and shouting from the Agent reverberated off the trees as Bennett fought to gain purchase on the man to get a kill bite in.

"Keep covering my back." Kaitlyn suppressed the attack from the other shooter. "Scan around in case there's others."

Spencer complied, trying not to focus solely on Bennett's fight with the Agent, though he had a good neck hold on the man. The Agent gurgled as his throat was crushed under the wolf's massive jaws.

Once the body stilled completely, Bennett remained crouched low and scented the air. Spencer's own heightened senses were straining to pick up any odd sounds. There. Someone was behind her. Her shoulder hindered her twisting around. Kaitlyn was still engaged with the Agent on their left. Could Bennett make it in time?

Don't move. He can't hit you around the tree. Bennett's firm words eased her worry. He would take care of the threat, she had no doubt.

Kaitlyn was covering her on the left, her Guardian stalked the Agent behind her, Spencer kept watch in front of her.

A shout was cut off short. Bennett had nailed his target. It was enough of a distraction that Kaitlyn's target turned her head at the noise. Kaitlyn siezed the advantage and dropped the female Agent with two to the chest.

"Damn. I'm out of bullets. I need to put one in her head so she stays down until we can roast her." Swiftly dropping the cartridge from her gun, Kaitlyn deftly grabbed another to reload her weapon when movement straight ahead of the females caught Spencer's attention.

Rounding a tree, another female Agent placed Spencer in her sights with an evil grin and a gun similar to the one the Agent had used to shoot the silver.

Panic surged in Spencer. She couldn't survive a head shot with silver.

Raising her good arm holding the gun, Spencer didn't have time to aim, just shoot.

Blood sprayed from the woman's forehead and she dropped to the ground, never having taken her shot at Spencer. Confusion raced through Spencer's mind, she was certain she missed. Something didn't make sense.

Then it came to her. The head shot was just like the vampire's, when the Agent in her house shot him from behind.

Searching the trees, Spencer's heart raced. Who took out the Agent? It had to have been one of the Guardians.

"What the fuck, Bennett?" Kaitlyn crouched in front of Spencer, frantically scanning the woods like Spencer was. "Who did that?"

Spencer sensed the big wolf moving low through the trees, hunting the mystery shooter.

A flash of dark clothing in the distance caught all of their attention. The figure, all in black, with a head of black hair, could be seen striding away.

Bennett gave a short bark and the figure, another female, wasn't far enough away that Spencer couldn't see her flip off the wolf.

"Don't worry, blondie. There's only two other survivors and they think she's dead. Your secret's safe with me," the female called over her shoulder. A shifter from the scent, she continued sauntering away.

Right, and I can trust you, X? Bennett's mental voice was filled with derision.

"I don't want her dead, now fuck off." The female strode out of sight.

There was something vaguely familiar about the Agent. Her voice tickled Spencer's memories, but she'd traveled quite a bit with her family and came across a lot of people. Where would she have crossed paths with another shifter long enough to recognize her voice?

The question was dropped as soon as she saw the pale wolf walk up next to her.

We need to get you to Doc Garreth.

Right, the healer. Yes, she did indeed need a healer. How many others did? "Was anyone else hurt?"

Not badly. No one was hit with silver like you. Let's get you checked out first and then you can tell us what happened. Bennett nudged under her elbows to let her know she could use him to try to stand. And she would take him up on that offer.

Kaitlyn headed to the Agent she felled to get her head shot in.

There's still a vampire out there, Kaitlyn. Eyes open.

So, Bennett was bossy with everyone, Spencer mused, not just her.

"There was a vampire that went up in flames at the house. Was there more than one?"

"Woo-hoo!" Kaitlyn gave Spencer an appraising look. "You took out a fanger? Oh, no offense," she finished quickly and sincerely.

Spencer smiled and shook her head. "I'm not vampire enough to be offended. And no, I think it was an Agent who killed the vampire." Spencer's forehead furrowed as she recalled how the Agent helped her and then apologized before he shot her with a silver bullet.

An Agent? Describe him. Bennett helped Spencer stand. It had taken a couple of tries. His sense of urgency at getting her to the lodge radiated off him. Did she look as bad as she felt?

"Tall, dark, and deadly. He even said he was sorry he had to shoot me."

What? He fired point blank on you and only hit you in the shoulder? Bennett's tone was incredulous.

"It sounds like Agent E and he doesn't miss," Kaitlyn said.

"Well, I tried to get out of the way," Spencer offered.

Wouldn't matter. If he wanted you dead, you would be. What are they up to?

"Shit Spencer. Doesn't hurt to have Agent X and Agent E protecting you."

It's likely the only reason she's still alive, Bennett added grimly. *It's like they were hanging out in town watching us so we'd go into overdrive protecting Spencer. We'll have to see what the commander makes of it.*

They made their way to the lodge, moving at the fastest pace Spencer could muster. She hurt; her shoulder throbbed and her strength was waning.

Bennett stayed in his wolf form, walking next to Spencer so she could tunnel her hand through his fur and use his support as they made their way over the uneven terrain.

Kaitlyn mentally reported the bodies to the others so they could gather them and throw them in the fire.

Spencer should mourn the loss of her house, but she didn't. Right now, she was glad to be alive, and if she didn't get to the lodge soon, that might change.

Spencer was weak and draining fast. Standing quietly downwind and out of sight, the large ruddy wolf noted her haggard walk, while leaning on Bennett. He spied on them until Bennett flowed back into human form to swing her up into his arms. She melted into his chest, trying to keep her eyes open. Kaitlyn followed them, studying their surroundings, protecting the couple so they could reach safety.

Pride swelled in the commander while he stayed in his wolf form watching the actions of his pack. This was why they kept going. All those years that their powers didn't work, the dregs of society draining any optimism of a decent future, and the steady rise of Sigma's power, he'd felt almost helpless against the wildness that threatened to take down his small pack. Now his boys were finding their mates, his pack was growing, and they would need every resource to not only defeat Madame G, but wipe out Sigma's presence in this area and deal with the corruption in their own governing body.

Rhys didn't come out here to haul the bodies to the fire. Mercury, Jace, and Ronnie said they'd take care of it while Rhys told them he'd clear the woods.

He didn't exactly lie to them. There were no more Agents after them, but there were still Agents among the trees. One of the Agents involved in the gun fight had taken off already, thinking their plan was a success and the hybrid had perished in the flames. With any luck, Agent E thought so, too, but he wasn't close by. Probably near the road where they had vehicles waiting.

Rhys was only interested in one Agent, and even after what he just witnessed, he doubted he would get any answers from her.

"Looking for me?"

Rhys swiveled his head toward the coy tone and there she stood, dressed all in black with her midnight hair swept to one side of her head, showcasing the shaved side. He wasn't feeling bitchy enough to change back to a human. Nudity didn't bother shifters, but his nudity would bother her. He didn't want to play games, he required answers, and while he doubted he would get any tonight, he sure wouldn't get any sporting an erection that strained for her.

Don't suppose you'll tell me why you saved her, X?

"Why Rhys, I have no idea what you're talking about. I was aiming for her, but Agent C's head got in the way."

Rhys wondered if his wolf could take on a sardonic look. *Are you going to inform Madame G the hybrid still lives?*

"I have every intention to, but dammit, I get so forgetful." She put her hands on her slender hips and glanced around. "What were we talking about again?"

What about Agent E?

"Nice guy."

She was so frustrating he wanted to howl. Rhys should be jealous of Agent E and despise the man for more than being with Sigma, but he didn't. The two Agents carried the scent of each other, and he'd observed them interact over the years. They were dedicated to each other, thrown together after being captured and forced to work for Madame G, but their intimacy didn't scream romance.

Why they didn't try to escape Sigma was only one burning question Rhys wanted to know. Agent X was a shifter, though he doubted she'd shifted for years. She could turn to any of the Guardian packs for help. She should turn to *him*, but instead they sparred and fought, sometimes even drawing blood. Rhys suspected it was more for show, although that silver crossbolt incident a few years back left a hell of a scar on his flank.

He couldn't fault her for her relationship with Agent E, but he had an issue with that vampire, Demetrius. A low growl escaped him before he could stop it.

"What's the matter, boy? Timmy fell in the well?" X crooned innocently.

If Madame G knows she lives, she'll keep coming for her. Rhys was pointing out the obvious, but he had to at least find out if Spencer had any chance at a stationary life. If she had to run, he'd lose Bennett, too.

"You'll have to wait and see what Madame G's little rumored oracle says."

Oracle?

"Mmm-hmmm. A little birdie told me he thinks the madam has a seer at her beck and call. Can't say she's always accurate, though." X muttered the last part, more under her breath than anything.

Who is it?

"Don't know." X sighed. "I'm sure if my little birdie ever finds out, we'll have another vigorous information exchange."

Fucking Demetrius. The growling started again before Rhys could stop himself.

"Down boy. If it wasn't the vamp, it'd be someone else. Madame G would make sure of it." X studied the ground, digging her boot into the growth, almost as if she was ashamed of her confession.

Rhys ground his teeth together, drawing blood as his fangs dug in.

How can you trust what he tells you?

X gave the most undignified snort, her brilliant green eyes flashing, and it made her sexy as hell. "Trust Demetrius? Are you kidding me? No, but he does have an itinerary that I think might conflict with Madame G's."

She left it unsaid that she had her own itinerary that conflicted with Madame G's and so passed information between them would somehow hurt the madwoman's plans. Maybe Rhys hated the arrogant vampire a little less. Just a little.

"I remember when I was little, my dad would tell me shifter lore. You know, about the ancient ones?" X became reflective and Rhys realized he never thought of her as anything other than an Agent. That she may have actually grown up in a normal shifter family before, according to Dani, they were killed prior to X becoming an Agent. "He told me about all the powers shifters can have, and how they've gotten diluted as the ancients bred with humans. But he said any shifters with premonitions or visions were always extremely fair in coloring. Rumor has it, Madame G was pretty pissed about a pale young shifter she kept to herself that Mercury walked out with."

Well shit. X alluded to the oracle being a female. They would have to get their young Guardian-in-training, Parrish, who fit X's father's description of a seer, talking about his family history, like his mother or if he had any sisters. If any of this was true, and that was a big if, it would stand to reason Parrish knew exactly who Madame G kept in her quarters.

A shrill whistle that sounded like it could be a bird filtered through the night.

"Oh shit, that's my ride. Gotta jet or I'll miss it. It's not good for a young woman to be out all alone at night." She jogged swiftly through the night. Rhys let her go, didn't move so he could watch her lithe form until she disappeared from view.

Chapter Fourteen

Three months later…

"You sure you don't want me to come with, just in case?" Jace asked.

Bennett had stopped in at the lodge to grab some supper. Jace was on kitchen duty and no one complained. That male could cook. Tonight was beef medallions with bacon wrapped shrimp. Cassie threw together a salad and grilled some potatoes since she insisted on a well-rounded meal. No one cared but the ladies, yet they all shoveled in lettuce and devoured the potatoes without reservation.

"You're off the hook, and I can quit having Cassie bitch at me."

Cassie gave Bennett a wicked smile. She didn't mind Jace helping Bennett maintain his playboy image going at the club, but she did mind the naked women and stench of sex he came home with, even though he didn't touch a single female, didn't sport a single hard-on for anyone other than his mate, and didn't enjoy any of it.

Actually, Jace told Bennett he did enjoy some of it. After Jace wove the spell around the women in The Den, essentially hypnotizing them into being convinced of everything Bennett should be doing to them but actually wasn't, Jace and Bennett hung back and chatted. They conversed about work, Jace's school, and Ronnie's acquisition and detrapping of Spencer's farm. When Weston got his turn to have the woman's full body of attention, they assumed the routine of turning their backs for privacy and talking about guy stuff.

Then, bonus, Jace went back to his cabin and Cassie's now heightened sense of smell from being mated to a shifter went into overdrive, and she had to lay claim to her mate all over again. Jace gave a shit-eating grin and said he was only doing his mately duties letting her have her way with him.

Bennett was relieved to hear that. Cassie helped him out a lot and kept trying, even as he pushed her away over the last year, and he would've felt like a steamy pile of dung if he was the cause of conflict in the couple's life.

"Good luck, man." Jace clapped Bennett on the shoulder as he left the kitchen to get cleaned up.

Back at his cabin, he showered and shaved, and dug a nice pair of black slacks and a slate gray button-up out of his closet so he could look like his usual clubbing self. Weston said he'd be at the club hitting up The Den if Bennett needed him. Politely declining, only because he couldn't punch the male through the phone for offering his services tonight, Bennett hung up on him.

Driving solo to Pale Moonlight, nerves were starting the get the better of him. Was this going to work?

***

Sipping her cheap beer, Sarah's gut was churning. What if this didn't work? What if she was made? What if she had to watch him pick up other women because this wasn't going to go as planned? Well, she put on her big girl knickers this morning, so she'd suck it up and play along. But it would suck.

That's why she was here tonight. Living in isolation at the lodge for decades, or going into hiding, with Bennett leaving the Guardians because he refused to leave her side, weren't options. So between all the brilliant thinkers who planned her death, they planned her rebirth as well.

When they decided her name and appearance needed to be changed if her rebirth was to be successful, Sarah wasn't sure she could trust the fervor in Kaitlyn's eyes. The Guardian frantically called Cassie to bring back a hair dye kit, "like the one we used for the great hair debacle of freshman year." Spencer got the impression Kaitlyn had once tried to go blonde and it ended poorly.

As far as a name change, Spencer became Sarah. Legally, she would soon be Sarah Young once she was officially mated to Bennett. Thankfully, her brother took over her farming for the year, and since Sigma knew he was her brother, it wouldn't seem odd. The store didn't know he was her brother, but he told them he was taking over as the previous owner had to relocate for family matters. Maybe a few years down the road, Sarah could openly take over, when the Sigma dust had settled.

First up in her rebirth, stay away from Bennett to keep his scent off her while he continued his pretend womanizing with Jace and Weston's help. Next, spend time as a wolf. A lot of time. Sarah stayed in the woods for weeks, running and hunting. Or rather, learning how to hunt as a wolf. The first jack rabbit about fell over on his back laughing at her attempt to catch him. After she left home at eighteen, she rarely changed to her other form because she needed to remain as human as possible. Before then, she was never a wolf long enough to need to eat like one. At least the blood from her kills was enough to keep her away from not only Bennett's blood, but Bessie and Tulip's as well. Ronnie took care of her beloved cows while he used them for his own blood needs.

After she came back to the city to live in an apartment Jace and Dani set up for her under her new identity, the girls threw a wine and hair dyeing night for her. Kaitlyn, with her love of shopping, bought new clothes for Sarah that were opposite of her country girl look.

Then Sarah went out one night and "happened" to bump into Kaitlyn out clubbing. The shifter pretended to never have met her and they made a show of becoming fast friends. Her new friend then dragged her around town to go clubbing for a few weekends. It was test to see if she was recognized so it would ultimately look less suspicious when she appeared at Pale Moonlight on a night when Bennett was around.

A night out with Kaitlyn was a wild time, but the Guardian shooed off every man, human or shifter, whenever they came near. "Back off, it's sexy bitches' night out," she'd shout.

Sometimes Cassie would join them, and once, Dani met them out, but only for a couple of hours saying her boobs were on call. Sarah hadn't gotten to meet baby Dante yet, but she heard enough stories to know that the little guy was going to keep the lodge exciting.

Finally, she was at Pale Moonlight to run into her mate. Sigma spies could report he'd met his true mate, a shifter from her scent, and they'd leave them alone…mostly. But at least they wouldn't target her for assignation.

A quick inhale, told her *he* had arrived. She missed him so badly. Their forced separation sucked. She missed him, missed her dog, missed her cows, and missed all those little kittens. Her heart clenched, they were probably close to fully grown by now.

Taking another drink, a gulp this time, she scanned the entrance to the club. He was already turning heads, women eyeing him, adjusting their clothing, hoping to approach him as he wove his way through the club.

His navy blue eyes skipped over each one of them, but he kept working his way through the crowd, as if he sensed someone he wanted more.

Running a hand through her shoulder length flaxen hair, she checked out her image in the mirror over the bar.

Not too shabby. Her hair flared up slightly at the ends with the razor cut she'd recently had. Her new shirt fit snugly, showing off her figure without too much skin, and overlapping her first ever pair of skinny jeans.

She felt like she looked hot, and so did a couple of other shifters who had sidled up to her at the bar and tried to use their bad pick-up lines. One asked her to look at his phone because something was wrong with it. When she asked what, he said it was because her number wasn't in it.

Laughing them both off, she nursed her cheap beer, waiting for *him*.

Finally, the blond looked her way, his deep blue eyes intense, but slightly amused. He imperceptibly raised an eyebrow at her appearance.

Fiddlesticks. Didn't he like her new look?

Moving more forcefully through the club, bodies literally getting pushed out of his way, he zeroed in on her.

Her stomach was going to flutter itself right out of her body. The strapping grace of his movements kept her mesmerized until he stood over her. Sliding onto the stool next to her, a Belgian ale was automatically set in front of him, a sign he was a regular.

Nodding to the bartender, he took a long drink while studying her. She mirrored his motions, wondering what was running through that pretty little head of his.

"What's your name?" was all he asked.

"Seriously, that's all you've got?" she countered. "I've had two other offers tonight that put in more effort."

Irritation flittered across his handsome features and he glared over his shoulder, searching for those who dared to hit on her.

"It's Sarah," she finally told him.

A half-smile tilted his lips. "I'm Bennett, but my friends sometimes call me Benji."

She was about to go on making small talk when he interrupted her. "If I had a nickel for every time I saw a woman as beautiful as you, I'd have five cents. Did it hurt…when you fell from heaven? Can I borrow a kiss? I promise to give it back. Know what's on the menu? Me 'n' you."

Sarah giggled and held her hand up for him to stop. "Okay, Bennett, you get an A for effort."

Bennett's eyes twinkled as he took her in. "You look good."

"Thanks," she said, unconsciously fluffing her hair.

His voice dropped low. "You look delicious."

Heat filled her at his tone. It'd been too long since she'd felt him close to her.

"Want to head out of here with me? Maybe grab something to eat?" Bennett almost looked nervous, like she would turn him down.

Their time apart during her identity change caused him to worry she'd reject him, being reminded of his promiscuous past now that any choice of future was open to her. She'd get him over that insecurity tonight and remind him that she didn't have just a shifter's scent, but also understood their increased sex drive.

"Don't you usually take your women to the back?" she asked, innocently batting her eyes. People around them who were regulars of any sort attempted to listen intently to their conversation, and she was going to make it look real.

Bennett actually flushed, his eyes flicking to the back where Kaitlyn had holed up with Weston after informing Sarah, "Dude's going to take the edge off for me."

"I don't get the impression you're that kind of girl," he said, almost stammering over the words. Poor guy thought he'd insult her honor if he took her back there.

"And what kind of girl do you think I am?" Sarah flirtatiously flipped her hair and passed him a questioning look.

"My girl. You smell like my girl."

A guy two stools away choked on his beer, sputtering over the bar top, coughing. The bartender stopped pouring his drink and stared at them, mouth hanging open. Sarah didn't get the impression much shocked the seasoned bartender. A few female shifters, close enough to have caught the conversation, frowned in disappointment. Bennett just officially announced they were mates.

"I thought you smelled like you had good taste." Sarah smiled, wanting to jump into his arms.

"What do you say? Should we find somewhere to get to know each other better?"

Sarah had a plan and it might not be a part of Bennett's, but it was vital to help him accept her acceptance of all he was. "No. I think I want to go check out those rooms with you."

Now the bartender was smirking at Bennett. The other shifters had gone quiet waiting to see if he'd take his mate to The Den.

"You're too good to go back there." Bennett said, quietly serious.

"Aww, you're sweet. But you see, Bennett," Sarah turned on her stool so her legs were inside of Bennett's and leaned on his thighs, her hands dangerously close to the impressive bulge straining against his pants, "I've heard about you, and if you're really mine," she walked her fingers up his solid biceps and wrapped her hands around his neck, pressing her knees into him, loving the heat in his eyes, "I want to see what all the fuss is about before I bring you home. Because as I see it, we'll have too many new places to fuck to come here again."

At her use of a bona fide cuss word, he picked her up and stormed through the crowd to the back rooms. Sarah would've laughed with glee at getting her way, but her own desire was rising, and now that he had his arms locked onto her, and she'd felt his arousal, she just wanted him to hurry the heck up and get them in a room.

Finding where a door was open and no moaning could be heard, Bennett carried her in and kicked the door shut behind him.

He was leaning down to kiss her and pull her shirt up when she laid a hand on his chest, stopping him.

"I want you to take me like you usually do when you're here."

Confusion filled his features, followed by disgust—with himself. "Why? You don't deserve that. You deserve so much better than me."

There it was. She could feel the last few months had been hard on him. It had been demoralizing pretending to be like his old self because then he could actually see the detachment he'd felt, watch as the girls were so easily fooled because he'd had so little to do with them in the first place. They scratched an itch, beyond that, he hadn't cared about any of them, not even enough to get their name.

"And that's why, Bennett. Before I met you, I've gone out looking for a quickie just like so many others in this place and in all the other clubs I've ever been to. It's what we do until we find our forever. So," she molded herself to him, her voice dropping low and sultry, "why don't you try me out and make sure I'm yours forever."

Indecision still plagued him, she could see the war inside of him. Fine, time to bring out the big guns.

She backed away from him, moving closer to the chair in the small room, keeping her eyes on his as she shimmied her pants down. His nostrils flared and the intensity in his gaze bore into her skin where he visually skimmed her bare flesh.

Sarah turned her back to him, kneeled, and leaned on the chair, arching her back, looking over her shoulder imploringly.

Jaw clenched, Bennett undid his pants freeing himself. His arousal overpowered the room, making her heart beat harder and faster, anticipating his entrance.

Kneeling behind her, his length prodded at her opening. She was more than ready for him, no need for any warming up, he could glide into her with no resistance.

Bennett sank in and they both cried out. It felt so good, so right, and it'd been way too long she'd been without him.

Moving in and out, he thrust over and over again, holding her hips tightly. She didn't need extra stimulation before the impending orgasm rose and broke free. Crying out his name, hanging onto the sides of the chair, her ecstasy brought release for Bennett. He made a sound almost like a gasp before he clenched his teeth and growled through his orgasm.

Leaning over her back, arms around her middle, they shuddered together.

"I almost fucked that up and roared the wrong name," he whispered into her ear. Yelling Spencer would've tanked their well-laid plans.

Her breathless giggle was cut short because he was still full inside of her, and his lips by her ear sent a signal down to her center where she was still wrapped around him, informing her they were not done yet.

Bennett ripped her shirt over her head and snapped her bra off so fast she was sure he hadn't bothered to unhook it. Dang, she liked that bra.

Thrusting behind her, she held onto his arms as his hands kneaded her breasts. It wasn't long before they were both close to a second release.

"Touch yourself," he growled in her ear.

A quick inhale at his suggestion and she moved one hand down to her drenched center. She could feel him, moving in and out of her. Rubbing her swollen clit, she moaned and threw her head back against his shoulder.

Bennett's breath came harsher, his grip on her breasts, tighter. Lowering his head to her neck, he kissed and licked the nook between her neck and shoulder.

Knowing what was coming, Sarah rubbed harder, Bennett's thrusts became more powerful, yet he held her closer. The first waves of orgasm began and she called out his name and heard him growl her new name before he bit down on her shoulder as he came.

Her mouth dropped open as ecstasy poured through her body, the mating bite enhancing every tremor, every thrust, every sensation the male behind her was giving.

Shuddering, her hands holding his tightly, she leaned back against him while he pressed forward against her. They were holding each other up, wrapped in their embrace, still trying not to tumble forward onto the chair.

Mumbling into her neck, "Do you mind if we go back to your place before our next round? I mean, I'm sure they clean in here, but…"

With a little giggle, Sarah agreed. "I can't wait to claim you, but I can wait until we can roll around without worrying about leftover body fluids."

"Will your neighbors complain if I make you scream all night?"

Reaching behind her to wrap her hands around his neck, she turned her head into him. "They can suck it. I won't be living there long anyway, will I?"

He gave her a quick kiss and nipped at her lip. "Fuck no. But I can't wait for the drive back to the lodge to have you again, so direct me to your place."

She tried to dress as quickly as she could. Bennett shoved her bra into his pocket, giving her a wicked look. "I can see how much you want me through your sweater." His low voice rumbled as he thumbed her nipples through the thin fabric.

Slapping his hands away and biting back a grin, she bent to pull up her jeans, then straightened and took in his appearance. Rumpled blond hair, navy blue eyes lit up with desire, and his clothing in a form of disarray.

"Has anyone ever seen you so…" She waved her hands at his appearance.

"Satisfied?" That gave her stomach a girly twirl and made her shine inside.

"Not as put together as normal."

"Nope." A smug look formed on his face and he grabbed her hand, twining his fingers through hers. "Come on. I can't wait to show you off before I keep you locked up with your legs wrapped around my waist for days."

Aww, he said the sweetest things. Her inner glow would light up the whole club.

The nerves were back as they walked down the dark hallway. She could hear the cries of passion from the other rooms, and was glad she and Bennett were walking out of that phase in their lives. The nerves were increasing as they approached the dance floor. They would have to wind through the throng of bodies and make their way through the bar before they could leave.

"We can go out the back," Bennett suggested softly, giving her hand a gentle squeeze.

"I'm just not used to having all eyes on me." She hoped he'd make the connection himself that she'd been in hiding all of her life, striving to be invisible. Bennett nodded in understanding and before they entered the chaos of deep bass and flashing lights, she added, "But I can't wait for all those lovely ladies to know you're off the market."

Bennett gave her a genuine grin, one she didn't think she had ever seen from him before. Swooning female alert: this normally gorgeous male was staggering when he truly smiled. She almost missed the dejected faces from hopeful females waiting for their turn as Bennett held her tightly, seeing her safely through the bump of gyrating bodies. For a little ego stroking, she also noticed some males disappointed that she was no longer available. But there was enough flesh to go around in this place for all the disappointed parties.

Wrapping one arm behind her, while still holding her hand, he led her through the bar section of the club and headed toward the door. Sarah didn't miss the shocked faces of the staff who were familiar with Bennett's history, not just with the club, but the rumors of his past mate.

Just before they got to the entrance, a large, imposing male stepped in front of them. A petite female came out the office door to stand next to him. Tight curls framed a delicate face, yet she radiated power like the male next to her.

The male assessed the couple with eyes a few shades darker than his smooth skin and especially studied her. Sarah didn't feel any threat from the couple, but she got the sense they were close with Bennett.

"My bartender called with the news. Congratulations." The male clapped Bennett hard on the back. He held out a massive hand for Sarah to shake. "I'm Christian, the owner of this fine establishment, and this lovely female is my wife, Mabel."

Sarah shook hands with the couple and tried not be intimidated. They didn't have to mention they were pack leaders, she could tell from their energy and confidence.

"I just had to come see for myself. It's nice to see you Guardians are collecting a fine assortment of females to keep y'all in line." Mabel's sweet southern accent wound its way through Sarah, settling her nerves.

"Before you two go, I know you have unfinished business," Christian shot them both a pointed, good-natured look, making Sarah blush to her toes, "but I need you to pass a message to Jace, and make sure Rhys hears of this also."

"Sure." Bennett was all business, but he didn't ease his hold on her.

"A shifter from Jace's old pack was in here, trying to dig up information on former employees of mine. I believe he was looking for Jace, but he didn't give any indication why."

"And tell that boy," Mable drawled, "it won't kill him to call once in a while."

Bennett gave her a quick smile to let her know he would do so, acknowledging how much Jace had meant to the couple, and to the pack, before he left to become a Guardian.

Saying their good-byes and nice-to-meet-yous, Bennett hugged her close and steered her toward his car. She didn't drive herself, instead had arrived with Kaitlyn, planning to leave with Bennett.

Sarah leaned into Bennett as they walked. She wasn't completely free, it was possible someone would connect enough dots and realize Spencer King did not die in the fire. But for now she was as free as she could be—free to work the former land of hers the Guardians bought up, free to talk to her brother, and especially free to be with her mate.

***

"Quit protecting your left side, it's obvious it's weaker." Master Dane Bellamy used his staff to give Parrish's left leg a good whack.

He was barely breathing any harder than normal, but the young male before him was sweating profusely and wheezing as he attempted to stay out of the path of the master's staff.

Both males were barefoot and in the training center in the lower level of the lodge. Commander Fitzsimmons had approached Dane a few months ago and informed him that Parrish might know critical information about Sigma. Not only that, they still hadn't gotten the male's history—where he was from, how long Sigma held him captive, and why he refused to speak a word.

Dane told himself he had been giving the teenage boy time to heal, mentally and physically. That was a lie. To be honest, he was avoiding the kid. His own personal life went to shit a long time ago, and investing all of his time and energy into a damaged future Guardian wasn't something Dane looked forward to. He'd done it before with past Guardians: trained them, and trained them well, dammit, nursed them through tragedies life threw their way, and mentored them until they turned into capable, powerful leaders. But he had failed a Guardian who had been like a son to him, and he had somehow failed the most important shifter in his life, his mate Irina.

But days after the commander got done telling him that he needed to make progress with Parrish, Bennett had appeared in the woods next to him where Dane often ran his wolf. He shook his head, continuing his instruction with Parrish as they were sparring, and recalled Bennett's words.

"So, uh," Bennett had started gruffly, not looking at Dane, "I never did thank you for rescuing my sorry ass and saving me from having to kill Abigail. I probably wouldn't have been able to do it, and she would've tried to get us captured again."

Dane had stood impassive, afraid to run Bennett off if he readily agreed, but the male had continued with a question he never thought Bennett had considered. "You gave her a chance didn't you? And she chose Sigma over me, right?"

Emotionless, Dane told Bennett the details of Abigail's last moments. Waiting for Bennett's face to cloud over with anger, or worse, grief, Dane was shocked to see sad acceptance.

"Yeah, so, it's taken me over a hundred years to get my head out of my ass and realize neither one of us did anything wrong that day. I'm sorry."

Dane was too damn proud to cry. Instead, he just inhaled deeply, tilted his head back, and let the sun shine down on his face. Then he put an arm around Bennett's shoulders. "We live a long time. Sometimes, I think it's because we wrap ourselves up in our shortcomings and get lost. We need that extra time to get our head out of our asses."

Chuckling softly, Bennett and Dane gave each other a completely manly hug, while the dust in the air made their eyes water. Yeah, that was it. When Bennett left, Dane had begun his run, flowing into his wolf form.

Considering what he had told Bennett, Dane realized he needed to consider his own words. Parrish couldn't sit in his suffering and be allowed to remain stagnant.

As soon as Dane had returned from his run, he donned his training clothes, grabbed his staff, and marched to the TV rooms. Shutting off the Xbox and TV, he faced Parrish.

To his surprise, the male hadn't looked righteous or displeased at the intrusion. He looked resigned, like he'd expected this day to come and would rather have it happen than dread its arrival anymore.

"There's a locker for you in the locker room," Dane informed him. "Go get dressed and meet me in ten minutes in the gym."

The boy nodded and pushed off the couch.

Dane had trained him for the past three months, watching the youth's physical strength and bearing improve, gauging his mental fortitude.

Parrish needed to start talking, whether he used his voice or hands, whether he was willing or not. It was time for some answers.

***

"So what are you wearing tomorrow?" Sarah asked Dani, as they were facing one of the security expert's many screens.

"The weather's supposed to be gorgeous, right?" Dani looked out of the corner of her eye as she skimmed through old news articles online.

"That's why we picked the day. My intuition told me it would be the last before a rainy stretch." Sarah couldn't wait for her mating ritual. They finished moving Sarah's stuff to Bennett's cabin, and she was getting plans ready for planting and purchasing more livestock, and even some chickens, for the hobby farm she was developing.

"And you'll be holed up inside getting a little mating frenzy on during those days anyway?" Dani asked wryly, making Sarah grin.

"You know it."

"Enjoy it. Ours was cut short because we had a little Madame G purging to do. But what we did get in was quite memorable." Dani flashed through the pictures, scanning the articles.

Sarah had told them as much as she knew about her dad's side of the family. None of them got the impression Sarah's death was as critical for Sigma as they meant it to be, so they tasked Dani with finding her kin to determine if there were any clues as to why a female hybrid would catch Madame G's interest enough to kill outright, instead of capturing and using her.

Unfortunately, after tons of research Dani, in her words, "ain't found shit." Sarah's family seemed non-existent. That would be expected of her mom, dad, and brother. But going back further, there was nothing on her grandfather or grandmother, nor her dad's younger sister, her Aunt Allie.

Sarah's heart clenched at the memory of her aunt. She wasn't terribly surprised her grandparents had maintained a secretive, low-key lifestyle. They'd tried to blend as either humans or shifters but hadn't needed to be on the run.

Flashbacks of barbeques where they would play backyard games arose as Sarah scanned the images Dani was flashing through. Sarah and her aunt always teamed up. Ronnie had been too little play, and Aunt Allie shamelessly cheated, using Sarah's youth as an excuse. Sarah's dad had such a soft spot where his little sister was concerned, he good-naturedly went along until they were all rolling on the grass laughing.

Then there were the tickle fights. Aunt Allie would pin down Sarah and Ronnie as they screamed and giggled, and she tickled their bellies and blew loud raspberries on their sides.

Smiling sadly at the memories, Sarah tried not to remember the day her dad felt the omen that spelled something devastating was imminent.

"Can you call the commander here? I think I'm getting close to something."

Sarah sent out the mental call since Dani could only notify Mercury mentally, and he was out with Bennett on a mission.

Sarah's brow crinkled as she saw the same town's name pop up in several articles. Had Dani finally narrowed down the state? Ronnie had gotten some information out of their parents to try to find the tiny town where her grandparents had resided, and where her aunt went to school. Sarah couldn't safely talk to them without endangering her new identity.

Pictures of young kids popped up as Dani's fingers flew over the keyboard. She stopped and waited for the commander to enter.

"I was hoping you two could look through these and see if anything makes your senses tingle."

Dani enlarged pictures of kids, mostly group shots of high schoolers at sporting events. "This should be the town where they were last living, and these pictures are around the same time Sarah's aunt would have been going to school.

The commander and Sarah spent a few seconds on each photograph, her leaning toward the screen in her chair, with the commander standing over her and Dani with his arms crossed.

One picture flashed up, it was grainy and hard to focus on, but when Sarah made out one face, she gasped.

Commander Fitzsimmons dropped his hands to the desktop, focusing on the same face.

"Fuck me," Dani exhaled. "Is that—?"

"Do you know my aunt?" Sarah was in shock. If they recognized her, that meant they'd seen her since that day, the day she was supposed to have been killed. She leaned forward, pointing to the citing of the picture. "Look, it names the girls in the picture. There she is. They used her full name, Alexandria, but that's my aunt."

"Your aunt is—" The commander cut Dani off with a grimness in his voice that gave Sarah the chills.

"Agent X."

Thank you for reading. I'd love to know what you thought. Please consider leaving a review at the retailor the book was purchased from.
Marie

RECLAIM
Book 3.5, The Sigma Menace

Master Dane Bellamy was once the commander of the West Creek Guardians, a pack of wolf-shifters charged with protecting local shifter packs. Over a century ago, tragedy struck his growing family, driving him away with a fierce need for revenge. But his return held a devastated, withdrawn mate who resented him for his obligation. Now, he's immersed himself in training the Guardians of his pack while he and his mate have become nothing more than roommates, until the secret life she's been living brings danger to their doorstep. Suddenly, Dane finds himself not just fighting to save his broken relationship, but their lives as well.

About the Author

Marie Johnston lives in the upper-Midwest with her husband, four kids, and an old cat. Deciding to trade in her lab coat for a laptop, she's writing down all the tales she's been making up in her head for years. An avid reader of paranormal romance, these are the stories hanging out and waiting to be told, between the demands of work, home, and the endless chauffeuring that comes with children.

Sign up for my newsletter at:
Mariejohnstonwriter.com

Like me on Facebook

Twitter @mjohnstonwriter

Also by Marie Johnston

The Sigma Menace:
Fever Claim (Book 1)
Primal Claim (Book 2)
True Claim (Book 3)
Reclaim (Book 3.5)
Lawful Claim (Book 4)
Pure Claim (Book 5)

New Vampire Disorder:
Demetrius (Book 1)

Pale Moonlight:
Birthright (Book 1)

Printed in Great Britain
by Amazon